Keep the
fairy tales
alive!

VOLUME 2

Edited by **Jeff Conner**

Illustrated by **Mike Dubisch**

Cover art by **Mike Dubisch**

SAN DIEGO, CA
2011

Book Design by Robbie Robbins
www.IDWPUBLISHING.com

ISBN: 978-1-60010-963-8

14 13 12 11   1 2 3 4

Become our fan on Facebook facebook.com/idwpublishing • Follow us on Twitter @idwpublishing • Check us out on YouTube youtube.com/idwpublishing

Ted Adams, CEO & Publisher • Greg Goldstein, Chief Operating Officer • Robbie Robbins, EVP/Sr. Graphic Artist
Chris Ryall, Chief Creative Officer/Editor-in-Chief • Matthew Ruzicka, CPA, Chief Financial Officer • Alan Payne, VP of Sales

Table of Contents

REQUIRED READING REMIXED

The Fairest of Them All:
A Symphony of Revenge

By

Sean Taylor

First Movement—Once Upon a Time

They were nameless, though they had no trouble distinguishing one another. Short and squat, they smelled like the caves they mined, but that didn't bother them. They had done so and been so for more than two hundred of the humans' years, and they looked neither older nor younger than they had a few decades ago.

The one who knew himself as the leader, and perhaps the eldest—it had been so long and who knew really—walked the tunnels in thought.

The woman, the human woman, was waiting for them at the cottage. No more than a cleaned-out cave by her standards, no doubt, but for them it was as close to a cottage as they could tolerate. Before finding her, he had simply called the place home, but she had named it *cottage* and because they loved her, he could abide the change of terms.

"Good day today, brother?" the one with the red beard said as he passed.

"So far," Leader said. "Enough gold to justify another day of digging."

"That's not what I mean."

"Oh?"

"You'll turn gray from the worry I see on your face. You've got wrinkles on your wrinkles this morning."

He laughed, a coughing sound laden with rock dust. "I'm thinking about Snow."

"We all do. She's quite a beauty."

He shook his head. "Not like that. Something's wrong. There's a darkness growing in her and I fear we can't stop it. It's an ill wind, brother, and I fear for her safety."

"She's fine. The Queen thinks she's dead."

"The Queen is not a fool. She knows more than we hope. At any rate, what she doesn't yet know, she will learn soon through her dark arts." He cleared the dust again and patted his chest with a rock-like fist. "Snow is not safe and will not be until her stepmother is killed."

His brother dropped his voice to a whisper and cut his eyes askance. "Are you suggesting…."

"I'm suggesting nothing, brother. Merely stating a fact. Whether or not it is our role to play the assassin, who can know?"

Redbeard shoved his stubby finger in the elder's chest. "Be careful what you say. She has eyes and ears all throughout her kingdom, even as far as these Deadlands. If you don't want a price on your head too, I'd keep my tongue from waggling, or failing that, cut the damn thing out to keep it still."

He laughed and stepped away from the finger in his chest. "At any rate, it's not a matter for today. And there is more gold to be found to keep our little Snow's neck lined with jewels."

Redbeard raised his fist and opened it. Leader did the same then clasped it, and the two nodded twice and let go.

Both turned when the tallest of their brothers, though still a stump of a man by human standards, tripped along the path toward them, panting and dragging his pick behind him.

"Brothers!" he said. "We found something you need to see."

Leader reached up and grabbed his brother by the shoulders. "Calm down."

"What did you find?" asked Redbeard.

"We're not sure."

"Not sure? Then why are you running like a cowardly troll?"

Tallest grabbed his elder brother's dirty arm and pulled him closer. "It's a mirror, but we don't know what kind."

"What kind, what kind," said Redbeard. "What a stupid brother. A mirror is a mirror. There are no kinds. They're for women to crow about their vanity and little else."

"Not this one." Tallest crouched toward his brothers' faces, his breath hot and sweaty in their eyes. "This one has a girl inside it."

The cave stank of sweat and urine, and she cleaned it daily on her knees, then cooked whatever forest creature the little men captured and killed for dinner on the way home from the mines. She sang as she worked, a melody she remembered from when she was a child, perhaps no older than five or six. It was increasingly difficult to remember. The years had been far too unkind since her mother's death.

Her father's second wife had been a beautiful woman, practically a goddess of a high order, but only on the outside. Inside her throbbed a heart of poison. She hated her stepdaughter from their first meeting, pretending to enjoy their time together and planning whenever she could events that would take the girl and her nanny away from the castle, leaving her alone with her new husband.

She'd grown up lonely, and no matter how they smelled or how atrocious their table manners, the little men had become her friends, and she loved them.

Still she shuddered.

She'd seen the way the eldest of them and the redheaded one looked at her across the table. She'd heard that dwarves remained unmarried and merely mated when nature called for more of their species to arrive. Like something wild, something that was more a part of the forest and mountains, not part of her civilization of culture and glamour and pomp.

But that place had forsaken her. After her father's death, her stepmother had grown more openly vile toward her, insisting on marrying her off to a distant prince from a nation of barbarians, so she had run away.

To retaliate, her stepmother had thrown the blame of her father's death onto her and labeled her guilty of treason, then offered a reward for her death.

"Just a little longer," she said to no one, gazing out at the reddening sun as it dipped into the edge of the world. "I wonder what we'll have for dinner tonight."

As she spoke, she walked to the row of beds sitting in the dark shade of the overhanging rock. Once there, she reached down to steady herself with one hand then sat down, her knees poking up even with her chest thanks to the small frame.

The door burst open and a small dog with white matted fur bounded in and leapt into her lap, pushing her back onto the bed. Her feet hung off the edge and touched the floor, flat-footed, and the top of her head pressed against the head rail. The dog snuggled into her chest and licked her lips and nose.

"Stop, Aspen. Stop," she giggled, covering her face with her hands. "That tickles. Stop."

Of course the dog didn't stop.

"And you probably tracked mud all over the clean floor."

She finally managed to push the dog off her chest and sit up again. Clean floor, she thought. Not very. Even freshly swept it was just a base of flattish stone cut out from the base of a mountain and etched with a grid to make it look fancier than mere rock.

The little men had done that for her. They would have been content with a hole cut out from a rocky ledge, but for her they had created a floor. A pattern. A little bit of culture and glamour and pomp. For her. The same reason her larger wooden dresser and bed were adorned with spheres and cubes and statuettes of dragons and harts instead of the simple blocks of their own furniture. And the same reason her top drawer was filled with golden chains and colorful stones from the mines and the rest with fancy dresses they had traded for with the villages beyond the mountain. For her.

They loved her.

And she loved them.

But that was no longer enough.

For any of them.

The faces were staring at her. Ugly. Wrinkled. Filthy. Prunes with noses, she thought. No. Rotten prunes with noses. She imagined that they'd smell horrible too if she could be close enough to fall prey to their odor.

But the glass that had been her prison for years was in this case a grace, protecting her from the trollish monsters.

In her father's kingdom, years ago, he had gone to war with the creatures, and ultimately run them off his lands into the mountains.

But her father's kingdom was long gone, lost for centuries in the world on the other side of the glass. Her family had grown old, died, rotted and nested forests in their remains while she remained a captive of a witch who had stolen her away and sent her to this land of nightmares and hallucinations.

"Alice," said a voice she recognized instantly. "What are those horrid creatures?"

"Long ago, when I was much younger and not younger at all, my father called them the darshve. He told me how they were creatures born from the sides of mountains and baptized to life in the blood of our ancestors. Monsters of the rock and greed."

She turned toward the voice and smiled.

A white rabbit, dressed in armor save for his face and head stood before her, bowing.

"What news, Ulysses?"

"Alas, none, Alice." The rabbit frowned. "I wish I had better news. But I've traveled as far as the ocean to the East and as far as the swamps of the Jabberwock to the West, and no one has any knowledge of another doorway into your home world. It appears that when the looking glass was destroyed behind you, that was the only path to your old world."

"No!" she screamed and flung her hands against the mirror between her and the darshve. "There is a way, rabbit, and you will find it for me. I will not be slave to this witch any longer than I have to." Alice turned and glared not at her companion but through him to the door of her chamber. "And when I do escape, she will die."

She glanced toward the wooden desk beneath the mirror. On it sat a book bound in leather. Ulysses caught her gaze and asked, "And the book?"

"Sadly, no. There are paths to and from other worlds, but none back to mine." She released a heavy burden of a breath. "Yet."

The air between them wriggled. Then rippled out. She touched the center of the motion and pulled back.

"Damn."

"Her?" asked the rabbit.

Alice nodded.

"I'm not going this time," she said and sat down on the floor, crossing her legs in front of her. "She can rot before I let her collar me again with her beckoning."

"But Alice…."

"Hush, rodent." Alice glared at him this time. "Leave me alone."

The rabbit bowed, saluted, then turned on his left heel and strode from the chamber. When he was gone, Alice gripped her stomach and doubled over.

"No …" she said through gritted teeth. "Not this time, witch."

But the pain in her gut became a fire. In a few moments she crawled onto her knees, then lay her face down against the stone floor. Her stomach churned.

"No…."

She pressed both palms flat against the floor and raised her face a few inches from the stone.

"I will not obey you."

Her gut twisted and bile danced in her throat. She coughed. Three drops of blood splattered from her lips to the floor.

"I will n—"

Her stomach opened, pushing blood and water and acid and bile and pain and fire through her throat and thrusting it onto the floor in a puddle of green and red and brown.

"One day, witch," Alice said, reaching to wipe her mouth free of debris and mucous.

But another churning sent her hand to the floor to brace herself as her stomach emptied its filthy contents into the puddle again.

A voice in the air whispered, "Mirror, mirror on the wall...."

Second Movement—There Lived a Princess

"What's wrong with her?" asked Redbeard.

"She's beautiful, almost as pretty as Snow," said Tallest. "And she's young."

"Where is she?" Redbeard again. "Is she real, or the mirror a conjurer's trick?"

"Quiet, both of you," said Leader. "She's in pain." He tapped on the glass. The girl turned to face him and retched a third time. "She's real. That pain isn't a conjurer's game. No one could fake that. Look at her face."

His brothers crowded him at the mirror and he pushed them away.

"One side," he said. Not waiting for them to move, he pushed them away from the mirror and traced his thick, calloused hands around the oval edges. He tried to dig his nails between the glass and iron rim. There was no rim, as if the glass and frame were somehow molded from one piece of material. But it couldn't be, he thought. As a miner he knew raw materials, and iron was as different from glass as he was from the human woman living with him and his brothers. "There's conjuring here, but not necessarily only inside the mirror. This is made and bathed in magic. This is no ordinary mirror."

The smallest of his brothers, a golden-haired one with a mere few inches of a beard, shoved through the melee to the front. "Let's take it to Snow!"

"To Snow?" he asked.

"Yes, she loves trinkets and jewels, and a magic mirror would be the perfect thing for her to use when she brushes out her hair."

The others sighed and oohed approval.

"This is not a trinket, brother."

"No. It is a magic trinket," said Redbeard. "And our brother is right. Snow would love us even more when we give her this."

Tallest puffed out his chest and made himself a few inches taller. "And with the year of maturing coming soon, we will need to find women of our own kind or find something more wonderful than mere jewels to woo Snow."

"Here, here," said the others, in a sort of off-unison.

"Quiet," Leader said and stomped his boot into the dirty trail. "I say this is a bad idea. This mirror is enchanted and until we know what it does, it is far too dangerous to remove from this mine. But, we are brothers, and we will do what we will do. Who knows what role even this cursed looking glass may play in the evil that rides on the air through our Deadlands? We will put it to a vote and we will play our parts."

He let go of the mirror and leaned it against the wall of the cave. It teetered twice then stopped. The girl in the mirror had disappeared while they had argued, he noticed, though her chamber remained in view. Curious, he thought.

He sat on his knees and drew two circles in the dirt. He poked two dots outside the top of the left circle and one dot with a line across the top at the bottom of the right circle. Then he stood up again and walked to the wall opposite the mirror. He raised his pick and cut several slivers of stone from the wall. Then he put the pick down and gathered up the shards of jagged rock. He walked from one brother to the next and handed each a fragment until he had given away six of them, then kept one for himself and threw the remaining pieces into the dark tunnel.

"You know our way, brothers," he said. "Cast your vote."

They formed a single line and as each walked by the circles, he placed his stone in one of the circles. Redbeard placed his in the circle with the two dots, as did Newbeard and Tallest. Stumpfinger dropped his in the other circle. Then Finder.

That made two votes for each.

After Finder, No-Talk dropped his shard into the two-dot circle, then Grunt-Mouth did the same.

Leader gazed at the circles. Four votes to two. His vote was the only one left. Not that it would matter.

He sighed, then grumbled and stepped forward and carefully placed his stone fragment in the circle adorned by one dot and a solid line. Then he turned around and addressed his brothers.

"Let it be as we agreed. When we leave today, the mirror will go with us as a gift to Snow. Whatever danger befalls us and our love, let it be on our heads."

"Here, here," said his brothers. Then they each shook on the decision with open palms and two nods.

After they were done and finally returned to work, Leader carried the mirror to the mouth of the cave and laid it out in the sun. He slipped out of his tunic and spit on the cloth, then proceeded to wipe the dust and dirt and mud from the mirror and the frame.

That's when he felt the symbols etched into the iron.

Old letters. Older almost than his own people. From just after the time of the great wars. The Dark Days, as the humans called them. His own people called them the Time of Great Adventure but even the oldest of them couldn't remember the time. Only that they had been free to live anywhere in the land, not confined to the Deadlands.

He cleaned vigorously for nearly an hour, passing the time with a tune that Snow had taught him. He had tried to whistle as she had tried to teach him, but he just couldn't get the knack for it, and had to suffice with humming, though even that was difficult for his throat and mouth to conjure. In his own tongue, the old stories and songs were immensely disagreeable to human ears, and he had refrained from making the noises while in Snow's company, but he did enjoy grunting and burping out a story from the old language in private as often as he could.

Although—and the thought struck him as odd—Snow's songs were growing on him. Far too sweet and kind for his race. He knew that. But still they were pleasant, and they seemed to relax him.

There was no hurry, and he let the job take him another hour before he was able to at last make out the symbols around the glass.

Only, he couldn't read them. Not only were they older than his father's father's father, they weren't in his tongue.

But neither were they in any human tongue he knew. And admittedly he knew them all. The need to barter had dictated that knowledge.

"'Tis a bad sign, it is," he said, then spit again on his tunic to clean the glass itself.

Dinner was ready when the little men arrived home, just vegetable soup this time, since her friends had returned so late from the mines. But they didn't mind, and they each smiled at her in an odd way as she greeted them at the door and reminded them to remove their boots at the door.

"Such a proper woman," the one she called Smiles said as he entered. With a thick red beard and an almost permanent smile, the name seemed to fit him. Not that he'd acknowledge for himself outside her presence, she knew. His name would change among his brothers as often as his beard or disposition.

The tallest came behind him and she kissed his head. "Good evening, and how was your day at the mine?"

He only grinned and looked away.

The one who took care of the others entered last and nodded toward her then bowed slightly. "We have a surprise for you after dinner, Snow," he said.

Another necklace, she thought, or perhaps a new gown from beyond the mountains. That's what had kept them today.

The gifts were nice, but so inferior to her trifles at the palace. Still, that was a world and a witch away, and there was no use letting it ruin her mood in front of her friends who worked so hard to make her happy.

"Oh?" she said, feigning an excited squeal. "Perhaps we should skip dinner and just let me see it now."

"If you want to," said the little one she called Grandpa because his blonde beard reminded her of her grandfather's portrait hanging in the hallway outside her chamber at the castle.

"No," gruffed the leader of the group, a squattish stump of a man she called Squash for no other reason than it seemed to fit him. He coughed then relaxed his voice. "We will wait. Our stomachs are empty, and food and beer will make the giving more enjoyable for all of us."

"I certainly can't argue with that, Squash," she said, curtsying as she spoke, then let him take her lean fingers in his stubby hand and escort her to the table.

Once dinner was eaten and the dishes cleared away for her to wash, Smiles and Grandpa grabbed her hands and whisked her from the table toward the door. They led her outside, the others following as a group. She couldn't get back without trampling through them, so thickly were they packed around and behind her. Only Squash stood off at a distance, watching cautiously as he smoked his pipe. The foul odor of the ground bitterroot was nauseating from even a distance, but she dared not say anything to him, as it seemed to be his only real vice aside from typical dwarfish issues with hygiene.

The group led her to the edge of the garden they had dug out for her. Leaning against the rock-hewn gate was a flat package about four feet tall and wrapped in a cloth tarp.

"Open it," they cried, almost in unison.

Except for Squash, who remained a few feet away, still smoking his obnoxious pipe.

"Okay," she said and knelt down to unwrap the gift. As she did, her skirt fell away to one side, exposing her knee and she noticed that all the brothers grew quiet at once. When she looked, they were all staring at her smooth, white skin. She quickly recovered her leg. "Sorry about that."

Just as quickly, the little men started to grunt and whisper and jabber with each other as she returned to the gift and lifted the edge of the tarp away from the top corner of the package.

"Hurry, hurry, Snow."

"Yes, we want to see your smile when you learn what we brought you."

"Hurry, hurry, hurry."

So she did. She ripped the tarp away and exposed the gift, twirling around with a flourish as she did. Almost in a dance, just for the benefit of her little friends.

Then she stopped.

Cold.

The gift.

It was a mirror.

A very, very expensive and old mirror.

Inside the mirror was a young woman, blonde, staring out at Snow with the same intense gaze with which she was staring at the girl in the mirror.

She'd only seen a mirror this extravagant once before.

Only once.

Nearly fifteen years ago.

In her stepmother's chamber.

It had the same girl inside.

But the girl hadn't aged a single day.

The girl, Alice thought, the girl, the girl she thought she'd never see again. The hideous little blessed bastards had brought her directly to the stepdaughter of the wretched woman who had imprisoned her behind the glass and left her to die.

Only she hadn't died.

No. She had instead conquered the people in that looking glass world and become the queen of her new domain. It had taken many hundreds of years and cost thousands of lives, but when she found the book and formed an alliance with the elder gods, she had finally defeated and beheaded the evil queen who stole the hearts of her subjects to sacrifice to the dreaded Jabberwock.

Captive to the Queen, the beast had not been native to the land, but a dumb offspring of the elder gods from beyond. And when they had discovered how one of their own, albeit it one not a god as such, had been enslaved, they tore the life from the land and left it parched and mostly dead.

But time causes all things to change and when the creatures from beyond had moved on, Alice merely waited, biding her time as the green returned to the soil and the fragrance to the air, and even the creatures of the woodlands and seas forgot of the darkness of the war and saw only the bright new beginning of their new Queen Alice.

Not only that, but she had also used her time in exile to befriend and nurse even that dumb Jabberwock until it would eat live rodents from her hand without so much as drawing a single drop of blood from her human skin.

It refused to leave with its own kind. It was for the best, she knew. Its presence in her court secured the loyalty of the people.

And she had reigned for a glorious epoch, it seemed, but even a kingdom isn't necessarily a home, she had learned, and over time, all thoughts of political victory had simply faded away, replaced by the singular focus of returning home to kill the witch responsible for her exile.

No queen could be slave to another and still be queen, she had said to her subjects many times, and for that, the witch would have to die.

And her own stepdaughter would be the sword to raise against her.

Only there was the matter of the runes.

Alice stared at the dark-haired girl, envious for a moment for her pale, young skin. Already thousands of years older than she had been when she had fallen prey to the witch, Alice's own skin looked as young as the girl's but carried the calloused tightness of years of struggle.

The creatures were helping the girl to her feet again. She had fallen aback at the unveiling of the cursed looking glass and landed in a disheveled heap in the dirty path. Alice laughed. Then thought it best to smile instead. No sense in looking maniacal toward the only person who had a chance of freeing her from the multiple lifetimes of trapped torment.

When the girl was up and steady she returned to the mirror and cautiously placed her hands on the glass. Alice nodded and placed her own hands opposite those of the girl. The girl gasped and Alice said, "It's okay. It's safe," though she knew the girl couldn't hear her across dimensions.

Using the frame of her matching mirror in her own chamber as a guide, she traced the outer edge of the glass where it met the iron frame. The girl looked at her, confused, and Alice traced the edges again, this time pointing as she did to the characters etched into the iron.

"Come on, little witch-child, don't be a fool," Alice mumbled, tracing the mirror's edge a third time. "It's not that difficult, child."

The girl shook her head, as if to directly counter Alice's comments, and Alice felt her mouth tense and her anger find a home in her brow. She forced a smile and reminded herself to be patient, that she'd waited for more than a thousand years and a few more minutes or hours or even days more couldn't hurt her further.

Alice stepped back and settled into her chair. How, she wondered, just how could she get through to this stupid girl and her hideous helpers?

"Ulysses!" she yelled.

In the chamber she waited for the thumping of padded paws. She was not disappointed—nor was she often—and within moments the armored white rabbit appeared in the doorway.

"Yes, my queen?"

"I need parchment."

"Yes, my queen." The rabbit stood up straight, as straight as a creature of his sort could, and puffed out his chest, pushing the armor out full and gleaming. "May I ask why?"

Alice crossed her legs and puffed out a loud, heavy breath. "This fool of a girl is as dumb as an ox, and can't understand that I need her to read the runes around the mirror's frame."

"Have you asked her nicely?"

Alice cut her eyes at the rabbit, one of the few of her subjects who could get away with such sarcasm. "That's why I need the tablet." She motioned the creature forward and when he was close enough she rubbed his head. "She can't hear me through the portal. I'm going to write her a message, you brainless ball of fur."

Ulysses pulled away and straightened his fur. "You know I despise that," he said. "I am the Captain of the Queen's Guard, not a pet for you to coddle and coo."

Alice laughed. "And I'm the queen you guard, Captain Ulysses, and the one who named you and set you apart from the rest of the forest creatures who grew dumb when the former Queen's magic died with her. If I wish to cuddle and coo you, believe me, I shall."

Undaunted, the rabbit said, "I will return with a tablet, Alice."

Alice smiled, sincerely for her friend, unlike the forced and irritated smile at the dunce of a princess she was dependent upon. "Thank you." She petted his head again, just once, and tussled the fur there. "And I promise to reward you greatly when I escape from this world and reclaim my own homeland."

"And in the meantime, my queen?"

She leaned back in her chair again, uncrossed her legs, then pushed up against the oak arms until she was standing. "In the meantime, my friend, I will return to the mirror and try to educate this illiterate princess."

"By your leave, Alice."

"Do they not educate young women any longer in my homeland?" she mumbled as she took her place in front of the mirror and watched as the girl and her darshve companions did the same to her.

Third Movement—In a Land of War

Leader gazed at the fair-haired girl, learning her face, remembering it and comparing it to all the faces he had made himself remember during his life.

There was no match, but there were faces like it, faces that were etched in lines of sadness and colored with despair. Faces that time had painted with pain and outlined in anger.

But there was also something of the childish nature in her stare. Something like a human infant's smoothness. Something that reminded him of a young hart taking its first steps.

There was a deepness to the face. But a youngness as well. An infant face with a world of age behind it. The pieces did not fit. Young faces were filled with young life. Old faces were the only ones full of oldness.

The fair-haired girl was not normal. She was….

He struggled for the word. He hadn't needed to speak it or even remember it for a long, long time. A word from the old language, one he wasn't able to translate into any human tongue.

"Atyanshvar," he said, surprising even himself when he spoke the word aloud.

"At yon what?" asked Snow.

"Atyanshvar," he whispered this time.

His brothers stepped back from the mirror. They squatted on their knees around Snow and nodded. "Atyanshvar," they said together, like a prayer.

"I don't understand," Snow said.

The girl in the mirror, the one who was atyanshvar, the only he'd ever seen, the only seen in the last seven generations of his people, the girl stared at them as though she were trying to understand them.

"What did you say, Squash?" she asked.

"It's a word from the old tongue. It means…." He pulled on his beard. "There is no human word for it. I'm sorry."

"This thing, is it the mirror?"

He paused for a moment. If he let Snow know the truth, she would be unduly worried. But if he kept it from her, she could be in peril unaware. In the end, he simply shook his head and said, "The girl inside the mirror."

Let her at least know what was transpiring. If he truly loved her, he should; he would not let her face fate unprepared.

"She is old, but she is young," he said.

"Atyanshvar," his brothers nodded and said again.

"Nonsense," said Snow. "You dwarves have gone soft from all the dust in the mine," she said with a laugh, then crouched in front of the mirror and touched its face again. "She's barely beyond a child. Can't you see well? I am her elder by four or five years."

Leader came forward to stand beside her, his gray-mossed head level with her shoulder. He said nothing.

"I wonder if it's a door, or if it's just a window."

The girl inside the mirror heaved her small chest and crossed her arms. She smiled, but the corners of her mouth crawled down.

"I don't like it," he said.

"Pish," Snow said. "I bet she's sad."

"What makes you think that?"

"All girls who are alone are sad, Squash. I've seen only that rabbit with her, and I believe she is trapped somewhere. Maybe not inside the mirror exactly, but somewhere, and if we can see her, we need to help her."

Leader let his frown curl upward to a flat line but said nothing.

"Don't want to be a hero?" Snow asked.

Immediately Redbeard, Newbeard, and Tallest surrounded her, pushing him aside. "We want to be a hero, Snow," they clamored. "We'll be *your* hero."

She stroked their beards, each in turn, and kissed each on the forehead. He noticed the askew glance Redbeard and Newbeard shared, and he knew then that Newbeard was maturing into an adult of the species.

"The rabbit returns," he said, stepping between the young one and Snow.

"What's he doing?"

"Watch."

And they did. The white rabbit hopped to the girl and handed her several pieces of parchment, then stepped away and waited at her side. The girl all but ripped a quill from a desk beside her and shoved it into a small vial of black liquid. She opened the book beside her and fanned through page after page until she stopped. Then she smiled, nodded, and finally began to write, stopping only to check the book or look up at them through the glass.

Her eyes, he thought. They didn't echo the smile that settled in her lips.

After a few moments, the girl tossed the quill onto the desk and looked over the parchment. She nodded twice. Shook her head twice. Then nodded thrice more.

She rose from her chair so quickly that even he leaped back a few steps from the mirror along with Snow and his brothers. Shoving the parchment against the glass, she blocked her own image from their sight.

"It's some kind of writing," said Snow. "But I don't recognize it."

Leader stepped forward. "It's one of the old human tongues. From the time before my father's father's father."

"Can you read it?"

"I can," he said.

"And?" she asked, the lovely skin on her nose and lips scant inches from his own stubbed fig of a face.

Before he could answer, the parchment was jerked away and the girl fell to her knees. She lurched forward, facing the glass, her hands hitting the stone floor of her chamber hard. She screamed silently but kept her gaze locked onto Snow's face.

Snow, of course, seemed unable to turn away, her own stare captured by that of the screaming fair-haired girl.

Without warning, the girl vomited up flame and bile, her hair falling forward to soak in the mess.

Snow screamed and as Leader and his brothers watched, her legs gave way and she hit the ground in an awkward knot of legs and arms.

"Mirror, mirror on the wall, who's the fairest of them all?" The words broke the air between Alice and the glass, swirling in the space above her in colors she hadn't known in her birth world on the other side of the mirror.

She looked up, feeling more animal than human on her hands and knees, hoping for another glimpse of the dark-haired princess.

"No!" she screamed. "No! No! No!"

Her stomach lurched and the pain and fire climbed up her throat and found its way to the floor a second time.

"I was so close! So damned close!"

As she cried, the mirror's image faded and the view of the princess and the darshve was replaced by that of a beautiful woman with golden curls and a bosom that heaved with every breath. She sat in a large antechamber, surrounded by male slaves of several races, wearing only loin cloths, collars, and bracelets of iron. More cattle than men. Fit only for their queen's whims, whether to love or destroy.

Alice fought the image and tried to focus her thoughts on the princess, but the more she fought it the more her stomach emptied the impossible concoction of fire and bile onto the floor.

After thrice more ejaculating the painful mixture, she finally submitted to the witch's will—"For the last time, bitch!" she said through gritted teeth—and the anguish at last stopped.

As it did, the witch's room grew clear and focused in the glass.

"—est of them all?" she asked again.

Alice steeled her will to stand and face the woman.

"Well?" the woman said.

"You are very beautiful, Queen of the Kingdom That Once Was Mine. But there lives one whose beauty surpasses even yours, one whose natural comeliness outshines all that the dark arts have done to augment your loveliness."

"You lie!" the woman yelled and jumped up from her stool. She lifted it and threw it at Alice, but it merely bounced harmlessly away from the glass.

"One day you'll lose your temper and break the curse that traps me here, witch."

The Queen turned toward her slaves, sweeping her hand, nails extending like claws, in one wide motion. "Get out!" she spit. "Get out now!"

The men exited as one, none apparently willing to remain in the woman's company.

"I cannot lie, Queen of All My Family Used to Rule." Alice pushed her lips into a grin. "You know as well as I do, witch, that the curse with which you bespelled me will not permit me to lie to you."

"Cease your prattle, girl."

"I'm almost your equal in years, Stepmother." The word tasted like poison as she spoke it. But it went out like poison too, as was her intention.

"Enough," the golden beauty said. "Who is this wench who rivals me?"

Alice leaned in so close to the glass that she could almost kiss it. The Queen did the same, and the two held the silence for a moment.

"Well?"

And now it begins again, Alice thought. She laughed before answering.

"I command you to tell me, Stepdaughter."

Alice smiled again. "You know it is the daughter of my stepmother's fifteenth husband. You know in your heart that the beauty of your stepdaughter Snow will never fall second to your own."

The witch shrieked. Alice nodded and watched the golden curls fade away.

Snow pulled the cabinet from the wall, careful not to dump the clay dishes and bowls crashing onto the floor, and looked behind it. The mirror was nowhere to be found. The darling little troubles had hidden it away from her after she fainted.

She had awakened from the heat of the sun on her face. Her skin itched and had been pulled tight across her forehead and eyes, burning slightly to the touch.

The sun.

It had been too high for morning.

No, morning had come and gone, and the little men with it. She was alone in the cave and had little time to discover the secret of the girl in the mirror.

So she ignored the cleaning and instead searched throughout the cave for the mirror. She had to see the girl again. To help her. To learn what the words on the parchment had meant. With any luck, to set her free.

She could not let the girl go through torment like that she had seen, not again.

She was in exile, yes. Presumed dead, yes. Living in a cave, yes. Penniless, yes. But she was still a princess, damn it. And she would act like it.

The furnishings lay across the stone floor overturned and in piles as she examined every nook and hidey-hole large enough to fit the mirror. She even checked the floor for loose stones that could hide crannies and caverns below.

Nothing. Not inside anyway.

It had to be in the shed, then.

So out she went.

She took out the hammers and axes, then the picks and shovels, buckets both with holes and without, animal skins too numerous to remember how many and lay them on the ground outside between the shed and the garden. Then came bags of seed and watering baskets, followed by wineskins and mostly empty barrels of homemade ale.

At last the small structure was empty.

But there was still no sign of the mirror.

Had Squash taken it back to the mine?

"Damn him! He had no right." She kicked the wall. "Ouch!" she cried when her toe stubbed the stone wall, and she lost her balance and fell on her behind.

However, instead of hitting hard ground, she landed in soft, freshly shoveled dirt.

"Those sneaky little devils," she said aloud, and pushed herself off the ground.

She walked outside, crouching to avoid hitting her head on the way out, then returned with one of the shovels, really more a spade for her, but it accomplished the task. On hands and knees, never minding the filth staining her dress, she dug until she reached a layer of straw and twigs. Tearing away the nest-like cover, she soon caught a tiny reflection of her dirty dress.

"Those darling, sneaky rascals," she said.

Inspired by her success, she tore into the rest of the straw and made a hole large enough to pull out the mirror. Heavier than she expected, she struggled to lift it, but got it high enough finally to prop it on her knees and waddle out into the yard like a duck.

The sun looked down squarely from the western sky and she knew that her time was short.

Quickening her pace, she lifted the mirror higher, aiming for her thigh and hip, but it slipped and tumbled from her hands, landing glass side down on the rocky ground.

Snow fell to her knees and cried. She had destroyed the mirror, and her only chance to help the girl trapped inside. She dropped her hands, clasping them in her lap, in the fold of her dress, and let her tears drain down the dirt and dust on her face.

She looked less a princess than a scullery maid, a cinder girl, a common household servant now.

After several minutes, however, she stopped and crawled toward the looking glass. If it wasn't broken too completely, she might be able to fashion the pieces together again somewhat and perhaps even enough to do some remaining good for the girl inside.

When she reached it, she took a deep breath and flipped it over.

The damn thing was still intact. Not even scratched.

"It's a magic mirror," she chided herself.

She looked for her reflection but the dirt was so thick on the glass that she couldn't make out more than a dull shadow of something through it. Desperate to see the girl again, she gathered the hem of her dress, spit on it like she'd seen her friends do, and began to wipe it as clean as she could.

She was greeted not by her own reflection, but by the image of the blonde girl. No longer in pain, no longer coughing up fire and blood and bile. The girl simply sat in a wooden chair, gazing ahead, smiling at her.

Snow waved.

The girl returned the gesture.

"What do you want me to do?" Snow asked.

The girl shook her head.

"I don't understand." Snow lowered her eyes, focusing on the ground. "I want to help you, but I can't understand you."

The girl began to speak, but Snow couldn't make out the words. After a few minutes, the girl wrote the symbols again on the parchment tablet as before. Snow again shook her head.

"I can't read that. It's too old."

The girl yelled at her silently and threw the parchment on the floor.

Snow looked away and began to cry again.

"Don't cry, Snow." A hand on her shoulder, stubby and squat. Squash. "If this is the role we play in events, then we must play them as fate prescribes us." He took Snow's hand and helped her stand.

"You're home early," she said.

"We never reached the mine today. No sooner did we cross the mountain path than we saw the Queen's army on the march. At least three hundred fighting men behind her and she rides a dragon at the helm of the battalion. We hid in the woods for hours until we were certain she had passed rather than lead her here. There's precious little time, though, until she finds this place."

"My stepmother's army?"

"She is coming for *you*, Snow."

Snow dropped to one knee. Squash rested his hand on her shoulder.

"The girl. She is telling you to recite the runes along the frame."

"But I don't know—"

"She translates them into an old human tongue from hundreds of years ago. I know it because my father's father taught me the old tongues. But most of my kind has forgotten them."

"So you can recite it?"

He took Snow's hand. "No. I'm sorry. It must be read by one of royal blood." He squeezed gently. "But I can help you recite it."

Fourth Movement—And She Lived Happily Ever After

No sooner had Snow uttered the runic incantation than did the Queen's army top the mountain. The Queen led the charge, sitting across the neck of her dragon, a monstrous black and gold brute with a wingspan of several cottages and claws like broadswords. Beneath them her army marched toward the Deadlands, their boot steps resonating in unison so loudly that they could be heard all the way to the cave.

Even with the battle still nearly seven king's acres away.

Leader didn't care, though. He was busy dragging Snow away from the mirror, which had begun to pulse like a ring of water, flickering in ripples of glass and light and color. After a few moments, the glass grew still again.

"Is that it?" she said.

"Sadly, no." He stood between her and the glass, facing away from her, puffing out his chest to guard her from as much as his squat stump of a body would allow. "Remember this," he said, almost in a whisper. "This was not the best way, but it was the only way to save you."

"I don't under—" she started, but stopped.

A hand emerged from the glass.

Then the crown of a fair-haired head.

Then finally, the girl herself rose from the mirror and stepped away from it onto the ground.

She smiled at Snow, then glanced down at the surface of the mirror. Leader leaned in but saw nothing in its face but his own reflection.

The girl didn't look away. "Farewell, Ulysses. I shall miss you, old friend."

He couldn't resist the urge to peak again to see what he was missing. His whiskers itched from the need to see. Still, nothing returned his gaze but his own confused stare.

The girl turned, took a deep breath, looking into the sky.

"Home at last," she said and strode toward Snow.

Leader held his ground between them.

"If you've come to harm her ..." he said, deciding the threat was just as effective if unfinished.

"Harm her?" The girl laughed. "She saved me from an epoch of captivity. I've come to thank her."

She took another step toward Snow, but he held his ground.

"What did she open?"

"Just a portal for me to return home. I lived in this kingdom long before you were born, not long after your people were created from the mountains. Before your kind was banished to the Deadlands."

"I thought as much."

"It was my father, little darshve, who drove your kind away and made the land safe for humans."

"That was many, many years ago. Why return now, princess of ancient times?"

The girl lowered herself and knelt so that her face almost pressed against his own. "Because, creature of greed, this kingdom is my home, and was mine before it was stolen from my father by the one who now plays at being its Queen."

"Your time has past. You have a new kingdom." He pushed his face so that it touched hers, and she wrinkled her nose and backed away. "This is no longer your world."

"It will be," she said and sidestepped him, reaching for Snow's hand. "Regardless, my name is Alice, and I am in your debt, princess."

Snow took her hand, and Leader glared at her. "Should I know you?" Snow asked. "I feel like I should somehow."

Alice laughed. "Had time not been stopped for me, I might have been your grandmother of many ages past. But as it stands, we will have to be satisfied being half-sisters."

He saw Snow's legs about to give way, and he steadied her.

"Sisters?"

"Yes. The witch who thought she killed you is also the one who stole my father from me. She killed him after she married him. Then trapped me inside the world beyond the mirror so she could have the throne to herself."

Leader could stand no more, and he tore Alice's hand from Snow's. "Enough. That witch, the Queen, comes now with an army to murder your half-sister. What can you do to stop that, Ancient Queen Alice?" he sneered.

She laughed again. "More than is needed, little beast man."

She pushed him aside and stood over the mirror, then recited a verse of runic tongue, and the mirror flickered and rippled again.

This time however, it did not stop.

Nor did a human hand emerge.

Instead a tendril rose above the glass, tapering into a mouth full of knifelike teeth, followed by another, then another, nearly thirty in all, and then a sinewy leg of muscle and visible bone, then two arms of similar makeup, each thin like tree limbs but taller than a full-grown oak, each ending in a tangle of claws long as Norse boat oars. Protruding from its back were two massive wings of thickened, dried blood.

When at last the beast stood completely in the world Leader knew as real, it towered over the cave and rivaled the mountain in height.

Leader and his brothers scrambled in the creature's shade for whatever cover they could find. Alice merely stood between the behemoth's gigantic legs and helped Snow regain her footing.

"Beware the Jabberwock," Alice said. "The bastard child of the elder gods."

High atop the Jabberwock, Alice watched as the foot soldiers of her ancient enemy ran for their lives. None survived, of course. Those who weren't trampled beneath the feet of the elder gods were gathered up by the biting tendrils and consumed alive, their screams blanketing the mountainside until only the Queen and her dragon remained.

She had tried to escape, flying away to the Northern lands, but the Jabberwock had been a mere trifle among the creatures of the oldest world, and kingdoms were but a footstep for the largest of them, and there was no place in the world she knew to escape their reach.

In the end, Alice simply waited for the elders to return from across the sea with the beast and the witch in their grip.

When they did return, the ancient creature tore the wings from the dragon and fed them to the youngest among them. Then they lay the beast on the ground before Alice and placed the half-dead form of the witch-queen beside her steed.

"What are these magnificent creatures?" the defeated woman asked.

Alice smiled. "They are my allies."

"They will destroy this world like they destroyed the one beyond the mirror."

"All worlds return to the green in time, witch."

The witch spit in Alice's face. "But you'll be long dead, girl. There's no magic here to keep you young."

"I've lived long enough, more than anyone should be allowed. It's enough for me to die in my homeland."

The witch shook her head. "I don't think so. You're corrupt now, just like me, just like your father would have become if I hadn't killed him."

Before she realized she had moved, Alice's hand snapped like a vine and struck the woman full in the face. "Don't mention my father, bitch!" she spat.

"Just like me now," the witch said again, wiping the blood from her lips with the back of her hand then tasting it. "You can't be satisfied with killing me. You have to conquer. Is that not what you've promised your allies?"

Alice looked up to see most of the elder gods already moving across the face of the land, some heading into the lands past the mountains and others walking toward the sea.

Someone tugged at her sleeve.

"Sister?" asked Snow. "Is it true? Have you promised our kingdom to these monsters?"

Alice grinned.

"I have. But I don't intend to keep that promise."

"You have a plan?"

Of course I do, Alice thought. But she said nothing.

"You were always a dim child, Snow," said the witch-queen. "You cannot trust your half-sister. Listen to the dwarves you've chosen to live with. They'll tell you."

Alice watched as the stubby darshve who had tried to protect Snow from her stepped forward. "We all have our parts." He pointed at the Queen. "Even her."

"Well said, little man."

Alice gazed up at the Jabberwock, her eyes seeing something she knew the rest of them couldn't see, her words entering places the rest of them couldn't go. Then she broke the stare and frowned at her stepmother.

The Jabberwock struck her with its claws, slicing the witch into three slivers of human pulp. Alice knelt down and picked up the first piece, the center cut, and cocked her head sideways. "Goodbye, stepmother," she said and tossed the flesh into the mirror, where it disappeared.

"You there," she said, motioning toward the darshve with a short blonde beard. "Help me, and I'll give you position and wealth in my new kingdom."

"I don't trust you," he said.

"Do you trust gold?" she asked.

"How much gold?"

"Newbeard!" her half-sister shouted.

"Enough." Alice stretched. "And human women, none so lovely as my sister, but the choicest females from lands far and near."

The little darshve stroked his beard for a moment, then looked at the old one, then at Snow, then back to Alice.

"And we'll be safe from those things?"

"Yes."

The creature looked at Snow again, then back to Alice.

"Make up your mind."

He nodded, and grabbed the left portion of the dead Queen. As he dragged it toward the mirror, the tallest of the darshve went over to help him. Alice watched as they lifted the flesh and tossed it into the mirror.

"Blood seals the magic."

She walked among the remaining darshve. "What of you, little ones? Would you prefer to live off the mountain dust or dine like princes in my palace with your beautiful wives from exotic lands?"

The others said nothing. But neither did they step forward to help dispose of the Queen's corpse.

Damn them, Alice thought. Very well.

She locked eyes on the beast above her. Asked it for another favor, and instantly four of the little men lay dead, gutted at her feet.

"You chose poorly, little darshve." Alice looked at the dead darshve, then to Snow. "There's only one way to save this world, my sister."

The girl said nothing, only shuddered behind the old one.

"You can call them back to their own world, but only from inside the looking glass."

"All of them?"

"All of them."

"How many can enter?"

Alice took another deep breath. "I love this home air. Even filled with death, it calms me and helps me remember the way the land used to be."

"How many, Alice?" Snow tightened her gaze and it seemed to Alice that the girl had finally found some courage. Far too late, but an admirable discovery nonetheless.

"As many as who dare," Alice said. "So long as they go before you. Once you enter or I throw you in, the portal will close. Blood seals the bargain, not just my stepmother's blood but also the royal blood in your veins."

The girl knelt on her knees and called out, "Aspen! Come here, Aspen."

In a few moments, a dirty white dog ran from the edge of the forest to her and leaped against her chest to lick her face.

"Good dog, Aspen." The girl gathered the dog in her arms and carried it toward the mirror. "I'll join you in a moment." Then she set her pet on the mirror's face and it slid into the glass as though it were water.

Alice sighed. "Happy now, half-sister?"

"You'll die a normal death now."

Alice laughed and shook her head. "I've learned a lesson or two from the bo—" She stopped herself. "Damn! The book. I've left the book."

When she gathered her wits after a few seconds, she noticed the girl squatting down and whispering something in the old one's ear. He nodded. Then they clasped each other's hands and stepped onto the mirror.

In a moment, all Alice's allies began to moan in a low tone that shook the mountains. Then they simply faded away as if they had never been in the land at all.

"This isn't the end," the girl said.

"Wait!" Alice said, reaching for them too late as they disappeared through the glass. She turned to the two darshve who remained. "I want that damned mirror hidden in the mountains again and buried beneath a rockfall. No, two rockfalls. She is never to escape." She tightened her glare at the little men. "Never. Even if she learns the power contained in that volume." She bit down on her frown. "Do you understand me?"

She was certain they did.

Snow stared out the window of her chamber at the peaceful green and blue of the castle grounds.

The winters in the new kingdom were moderate, with little to no snow, and the temperatures remained just warm enough to enjoy the cold without freezing, but it wasn't home.

Back home, the trickster, the conniver, Alice, sat in her father's castle, entertained guests in her father's banquet hall. But that wouldn't last. It couldn't. She would see to that. The ancient leather book Alice had left behind would help her, even if she couldn't yet comprehend it. But she had time to learn.

Footsfalls thumped softly behind her.

"Snow?"

"Squash?" she asked. "How was the hunt?"

"Productive. I must admit that I enjoy this new land. And Aspen delights in the fields around the castle. He's like a pup again."

"But it's not home," she said.

"Alas. It is not."

"What did you bring us?"

"Four harts and a boar. Enough to feed all the castle servants well."

Snow nodded. "Tell the cook that I will prepare the stew tonight. I've missed cooking for someone all these years."

"I will," Squash said and turned to go.

But he stopped when she cried out.

"Again?" he asked.

She nodded.

"Don't fight it."

She shook her head. "I'll always fight *her*."

The pain in her gut twisted and burned, and her throat constricted.

The air above her rippled and spoke in the hateful voice of her half-sister. "Mirror, mirror on the wall...."

Twilight of the Gods

By

Chris Ryall

"Lie to a liar, for lies are his coin; Steal from a thief, for that is easy; lay a trap for a trickster and catch him at first attempt, but beware of an honest (wo)man"

Arab proverb

PREFACE

I'd never given much thought to how I would die ... because I never had to. My fate was written by any number of foolish scribes who put pig's blood to parchment to tell of the coming of Ragnarok that we gods will soon face.

For those of you mortals who haven't yet sat around a campfire and heard those tales, *Ragnarok* means "the twilight of the gods." As in, the day the sun ceases to shine on us and you humans are forced to find some other—lesser—group of deities upon whom to cast your prayers.

That said, it tends to make you rethink what you know about your impending fate when you unexpectedly find yourself staring down the business end of a sword, as I now was.

She pulled me close, her blade poking a bloody kiss into the underside of my jaw. She stared at me with those cold eyes of hers. It appeared likely to me now that my time would come sooner than was written. I suppose, all things considered, it's better at this point in my life to perish in the arms of a passionate woman than it is to do so in the flaming conflagration those annoying poets go on about.

Still, had I known then what I know now, I never would've come here to Jotunheim in the first place.

Oh, who am I kidding? I always knew it would go down exactly this way. I made *sure* of it, in fact. Your dreams are what you make of them, after all, and my foolish dream of finding love was always going to lead me to this.

The huntress drew back her sword, its perfectly honed blade reflecting a silvery line across its intended target—my neck. I suppressed a yawn so as not to embarrass her. Death can be so tedious. And not much is worse in the eyes of Loki than tedium.

1. THIRD WINTER

Before I get to that sordid business, let me back up a bit. My father offered to drive me there in his chariot. It wasn't so much that he wanted to personally escort me out of town as much as he just needed me to leave Asgard proper under my own power while that was still an option.

It was to the frigid wasteland of Jotunheim that I was now being exiled—an action that he assumed brought with it feelings of great horror for me.

I loved the golden spires of Asgard, but my presence here was no longer working for me, or for the general populace. They wished me politely removed for a time, as my father explained.

"Loki," my father said to me, "I must spirit you away from Asgard in the darkness of nightfall. For if brave, all-hearing Heimdall becomes aware that you still reside within these walls, he will pull your entrails from your body, tie them to my ravens' wings and send them a-soar. And I shan't blame him in the least."

That was why my father was the leader of all Asgard—his ability to put a positive spin on dire events.

My father stared at me. His one remaining eye was likely looking me up and down, filled with its usual mix of pity and remorse-tinged loathing. This time, I didn't notice, because it was the ocular cavity where his other eye used to occupy space that was truly troubling me. My father once plucked out that offending eye in what I consider to be a misguided quest for knowledge. After all, I venture to say that the knowledge he received upon removing the orb was something along the lines of "don't pull your own eye out, fool; it hurts like hell!"

My one-eyed father had his other son, my half-brother, constantly by his side, so what need had he for me now? We don't look alike, my father and I, and not just because I have two good eyes with which to see. We're not blood relations, he and I. Heimdall, the miserable oaf, Asgard's sentry, liked to spread vile stories that I am actually descended from two malicious frost giants, and ended up in Odin's care after he slew my real parents in battle.

In addition to Heimdall, who seems to have taken it upon himself to report my misdeeds to my father, my lunkheaded step-brother Thor also seeks to curry favor with Odin. And since he *is* the fruit of my father's well-traveled loins—I have been feeling like naught but an unwanted burden.

My dear father, king of the gods tho' he may be, likes to feel needed, and it's Thor who truly needs the supervision and help. Thor would likely forget to eat were not my father there to provide sustenance. This is not a smart lad I'm speaking of. Whereas I am an entity unto myself, dependent on no man or god. But still....

"I've been wanting to leave for a while, father." I had practiced this speech since the recent incident that really turned opinion against me, and I was starting to believe it myself. "It's my *dog* who raises my concern—I don't want to leave him here. He needs me, that pup. Can I—"

"It is no longer a question of your *wants*, child. Remaining within these walls will result in your immediate death and dismemberment, and I'd prefer that not happen under my auspices."

"Dismemberment, *too*? Why is everyone so mad, father?"

"My son, need you ask? The *brightest* of us has been extinguished through your misdeeds."

My father had a way of cutting to the quick.

"You must go. But I will watch over you from afar," he said. "Be it as a hawk, or a bear or—"

"Or a rutting pig, my father? Or ... no, I forget myself, mother is doing her dutiful best to finally curb your rutting, isn't she?"

I could suddenly see enough distaste for me in his one eye to be glad that its mate was no longer perched on the other side of his nose.

We departed that evening. Forgoing his sky-chariot, my father chose instead to spirit me away in the guise of a snow owl, and he clutched me, now transfigured into a common rat (not *my* choice of animal, mind you), in his talons. (Also, this was not my preferred way to travel, let me tell you.)

As we traversed the night sky, my father remained silent. I noticed the temperature dropping considerably. In the sky, I mean. My father's own temperature was already matching the frigid air before we even took flight.

"Father, might we stop for some warmth? My teeth are chattering, and this rat-body isn't equipped for...."

"Your teeth chatter like the rodent you have become, my son. Now remain quiet."

Quiet wasn't in my nature whether I was rat or god, however.

"Father? The cold ... it persists beyond the norm, doesn't it? We should be basking in a warm spring evening for this flight, should we not?"

"Aye, Loki, that we should." He squeezed my rat-form a little tighter. Perhaps unconsciously. But likely not. "It would indeed be a renewed spring world for us all, had your machinations not led us to this point.

"You, my son, have brought on Fimbul Winter. Ragnarok cannot be far away now."

Fimbul Winter. That is, winter lasting for three seasons in a row, without break. Winter so cold, it threatens to crack the nine worlds in half. The ever-winter. The end-storm. The—

"Loki, are you listening?"

"Of course, father. Cold, snow, Armageddon. Got it." I think he kept talking but really, with the cold numbing my tiny ears and still more talk of our pre-ordained fates, who could be expected to properly listen?

"I was saying, Loki, that if you gaze across the horizon, you will see the world-tree, Yggdrasil. Its branches extend into the heavens and across this world, as well as others. Perhaps soon you will sit under its all-encompassing coverage and reflect upon what you have done. Perhaps there, you will learn what I seem unable to teach you."

"Possibly, father. Or perhaps I will instead become a beaver and eat through its braaaaaanches—!"

My father released me from his talons suddenly, his wings never beating any slower as he did so. I dropped down in the night sky, the heavy clouds through which I fell coating me with a layer of ice that only helped increase my speed.

My father the one-eyed owl was already out of sight when I struck the ground, and hit it hard, I did. But at least the impact jarred loose all the ice and soot stuck to my ratty fur.

Before changing back to now-bruised human form, I lay on the ground, letting my bones and muscles stitch themselves back together. My flattened lungs gasped for deep breaths of air. I was a rat, I was bruised and dirty, and I was alone in the cold, dark night.

So it was that Loki the trickster-god came to Jotunheim. Just in time for the new school year to begin.

This frozen area of the eternal realm was where I was now stuck—an action that I took to with equal parts horror and anticipation.

I enjoyed living in Asgard, the grandeur and pomposity of it all. I was enamored with the extreme seriousness with which most of my godly cohorts went about their day. I loved deflating those pompous balloons. But I also felt alone inside its stately walls.

"Loki," my father spoke to me through one of his ravens, which now took perch upon my shoulder—abandoned by him though I had been, he couldn't just sever the golden string entirely and loose me on snowy Jotunheim without parting words—"though you be not born of my blood, still are you my son. Still will I care for you from afar."

"Still will you use your bird to make sure I don't pull a fast one and leave this frozen wasteland, father. I know well how you work."

"Dearest Loki," the raven said again in its best bird-like approximation of my father's stentorian tones, "I helped you avoid the reckoning that you were due. But the forces you have set in motion cloud the mood here every day, even as the doom-clouds gather in the sky."

"Yes, yes." Now he had birds trying to make me feel guilty?

"You misunderstand. My message is two-tiered. The first thing I want to impart is that I need the time you spend in Jotunheim's school system to be productive; you need to learn humility, honor, and respect."

"I hope those classes are offered here, All-Father."

"And the second thing I need you to know is that there may not be an Asgard for you to return to when your lessons are done."

Well, this was an interesting tactic to take. "Packing up and moving where I can't cause any more mischief, father?"

Have you ever heard a raven emit an exasperated sigh? I just did. "The forces in fiery Muspelheim are gathering, Loki. Fimbul Winter is but the beginning."

"From there, I'd expect the cold of this never-ending winter to dampen even the spirits of Muspelheim fire-demons, my father."

"Always levity from you when gravity is needed. I could no longer protect you from retribution were you to remain in Asgard, and now, I must devote my energy toward preventing the impending conflagration. In short, I cannot keep watch over you. You will be alone, my son."

We said our goodbyes. The bird resisted my attempts to kiss it on its lips, in part perhaps because it possessed no such lips. As it flew off, my father's bird-words rang in my head—I was alone. Again, as it ever was.

Well, my dog would join me soon. Hopefully under nicer transport from Asgard than I had myself.

I took refuge in a nearby barn and pondered my situation. The surrounding meadow and its wild horses grazing nearby would suit my dog just fine once he was sent along to me.

Removed as I was from Asgard now, away from the familiar faces and regular opportunities to scheme against those windbags, I began to feel more alone than I ever had before. And one never wants to enter a new school fully alone, not even the great trickster-god himself.

Jotunheim High School had a total of three hundred and thirty-six—now thirty-seven—students; the number of Asgardian schoolchildren upon whom I could visit my many pranks had numbered into the thousands. Also, I knew those children; I knew their parents. I likely out-schemed generations of the same family. Here, however, I knew not what to expect. I would be the outsider to these students. If I was lucky, that is. Worse still would be for my reputation—and my recent misdeed, which so many in Asgard found unforgivable—to follow me here.

I knew from my earliest days of consciousness that I would never fit in amongst the Asgardians. Physically, I could alter my form to adopt the typically bulky form of your average god-son. But mentally, it was apparent I'd never be one of them. Instead, I took comfort in the goat-meadows; as a fish in the lakes and streams; in my time soaring the heavens and excreting upon the heads of the self-important gods in my midst. But among others my age who dwelled within the realm eternal—I always felt removed from them. I certainly never befriended anyone there.

Walking around my new surroundings, I happened upon a frozen patch that reflected my own haunted visage back to me. I looked sallow, pale. So no problems there, anyway. But my heart—the very organ that many ... okay, most ... accuse me of not possessing—beat with a certain ache I'd not noticed before.

Add to that the nagging feeling in my head that the idea of an outsider such as me ever knowing true love was nothing but folly, and it becomes clear why a single tear escaped my eye that night, rolled down my cheek, and froze there (damned Fimbul Winter). The hollow ache in my heart persisted all night.

And the pain was just beginning.

I arrived at the school early the next morning. This is because the hours I keep are my own, and I refuse to be told when to arrive anywhere. Which occasionally leads to awkward moments where I arrive too early, or even worse, on time, without aiming to do so.

I went to the school's administration office, where a heavyset woman with a braid the thickness of my forearm looked me up and down.

"I don't recognize you. New one, then, yah?"

"Yes, yes," I said, taking sudden interest in my boots as I felt her eyes looking me up and down.

She handed my class assignments to me and I walked off, paying no heed to her parting platitudes and empty words about how I should do my best to fit in. Were I not trying to keep away the attention of the Asgardians who wanted my head, I might well have fit my sword in her back. Had I been able to keep my sword, that is. She confiscated it from me before I headed off, telling me that weaponry was allowed only in the hands of the teaching staff, not the students. Already this school's rules were proving tough to take. Perhaps I would have been better served to follow my original plan of disguising myself as a fish and swimming in streams to avoid the vengeful eyes of Heimdall and his ilk back home.

My first class was Olde English. The teacher spat out my name with distrust as she read it upon my class assignment. "Loki Odinson." I felt all eyes from the other students on me. O, for the ability to use my magicks so that I might transform their eyes to stones, that I might then cast each and every one into the river.

Our reading assignments in the class were handed out. As I exited the class, I assumed that the minor trickery required for me to turn it to smoldering ash in my palm would raise no suspicions.

A voice surprised me as I brushed the ashes from my hand. "Hey, the teacher called you 'Loki Odinson,' right? Hi, Loki Odinson, I'm Eilif!"

Gods help me. Upon turning to face this intrusive wretch, I saw that he had to be a departed soul who resided in Valhalla, the land where dead warriors were welcomed upon their passing. Eilif was obviously here as part of the school's exchange-student program. His face and hands were disfigured from burns he no doubt suffered in his final battle upon this plane. In Valhalla, such a visage would appear healed, for the warrior's shade was returned to its most beautiful upon acceptance into the hall of the dead. But here, in this school, his appearance was distracting and rather repulsive.

"Just 'Loki,'" I said, doing my best to avert my eyes from his scarred countenance. "Although I'd prefer you not only not call me by name but also forget my name and countenance altogether."

"Hah! Good one. Anyway, I'm Eilif!"

"Yes, so it would seem, you are."

"They sometimes call me Eilif the Lost, but I'm not that bad with directions. I mean, the fire I walked into seemed like it sprung up out of nowhere. Lots of fires have sprung up lately. Seems like ever since beautiful Balder the Brave was killed by recent treachery that fire and pain have been around every corner. Well, maybe not fire here, since it's so cold and snowy and cloudy but still, wow, yeah."

If Eilif's previous utterance were to be transcribed, let me just tell you that there is no way a scribe could portray the speed with which one word followed another. Eilif needed to earn his nickname and get lost ere I pluck his tongue from his charred face and feed it to a toad of nondiscriminating palette.

The droning timber of his voice quickly became naught but an unintelligible buzzing in my head as it soon was apparent that he required neither response nor acknowledgment in order to keep merrily prattling on.

Eilif and I shared another class, and his incessant talking continued throughout. Following that, we headed in separate directions and I thought I was through with him. But unfortunately, as I later made way to the many spits where fire-roasted lunch awaited us, he approached me once again.

It had been a long day already and not yet half-done, and the constant feeling of scorn from teachers and students alike had been mentally exhausting. I craved neither food nor the companionship of Eilif, who was as interested in explaining to me the breed of goat we were to consume as I was in trying to tune out his voice.

It was then that my aches, my hunger, my loathing for both myself and all others ... all of these discomforts left my body in a flash, for it was there in the lunchroom at that moment that I first noticed *them*. A group of mysterious strangers across the lunching area. The rest of the world seemed to turn insubstantial and gray in comparison to what I now saw.

There were four students all hunched together, keeping their distance from everyone else. Every one of them possessed a near-translucent skin tone, as pale as anyone yet to be spirited away to Valhalla's halls. Their hair colors and body types varied greatly, yet there was something about them that made them all seem the same. I couldn't quite put my finger on it. Had I been able to, I would've saved myself the grief to come.

The smallest of them all stood a foot taller than anyone else within sight. They all had dark eyes, with deep shadows under those ebony eyes. I was nigh mesmerized by what I saw, but it wasn't because of their overall appearance.

No, I stared because their icy faces were inhumanly beautiful, like visions glimpsed in an oracle's reflecting pools. One in particular, a female. They all bore the visage of godlike beings. Yet I was myself a northern god, and familiar with the surrounding pantheons. Which begged the question ...

"Who *are* they?" I said in a breathless tone.

By this time, Eilif and I had been joined by other students he knew. One of them was a female fire-demon named Surty, another a lowly Viking child. They ignored my query; instead, Surty spoke at length about being here in Jotunheim as part of the advance scout for some invasion or other. If I had a gold coin for every time I heard someone talk about their intent to invade somewhere, I could swim in a pond-full of gold. Besides, I could not be bothered to listen to her when there was a much more captivating scene displayed in front of me.

Surty changed her tactic, moving from talk of impending war to a subject that actually interested me—the answer to my question of just who was the bedeviling creature in front of me. She said, "They're the Geirrods. Those blondes are Grid and Griep, the thin one is Porr, and that brunette," she paused for effect, "is Gjalpa."

I ran the name through my head. *Gjalpa.*

"They all live together with Geirrodr and his wife in the northern shadow of Yggdrasil."

"They don't look related," I said.

"Oh, they're not." Surty had clearly grown bored with this conversation, and she absentmindedly melted the leftover chicken bones in her grasp as she spoke. "Some say they moved here years ago. Some say they've always been here. Geirrodr adopted all of them, wherever they're from."

As we spoke, I glanced again at the group of over-tall strangers. From across the room, Gjalpa appeared to turn her head and stare at me. Not just look in my direction, but into mine own eyes. Is that ... is that even possible, that she should notice an outcast such as I?

Well, let me correct that—of course it's possible that she would notice me. For am I not still Loki? But regardless of my opinion of myself, I quickly turned away. When I looked back a moment later, she and her group were gone.

"Time to get going," Surty said. "Got to study. Schoolwork before making war." She wandered off with her friends, leaving me alone with my thoughts. And Eilif.

"Where you headed next, lemme see!" He grabbed my class schedule from my hand. "Ahh, you've got Metallurgy next, same with me. C'mon, I can walk you there. I'll show my nickname isn't accurate any more! Eilif the *Found*, I am!"

I prayed that Heimdall didn't hear the sound of my eyes rolling from here to Asgard, but it wasn't out of the question.

In the Metallurgy class, my luck improved when Eilif drifted away to sit with others he knew. For an anonymous and disfigured dead Viking on loan to the school from Valhalla, he certainly seemed to know a vast array of people. He took a seat in the back of the room, his endless prattle wafting away from my ears as I headed toward the one remaining open seat. It was then that I noticed the person occupying the seat next to where I was headed—*Gjalpa Geirrod*.

I took my seat next to her. As I sat, I turned to look at her. At her shoulder, anyway—her actual head sat at least another head's length above mine. These were not small people, the Geirrods.

She turned away from me, and her frosty demeanor was palpable.

As the teacher, a hideous dwarf who I could scarcely stand to lay eyes on, began his lesson, I noted that Gjalpa's hand was frozen in a fist. The waves of coldness continued to emanate from her. Had I somehow so wronged her with my furtive glances earlier that she was filled with cold loathing for me? Or was this normal behavior for her? My reputation, my recent misdeed in Asgard ... those could not have followed me here so quickly, could they?

I dared not speak to her until she relaxed her fist.

This continued on for the duration of the class. The disgusting dwarf spoke much, danced around animatedly as he spoke of smelting steel, and did his level best to keep the class engaged. I paid his foul self no attention whatsoever. Despite the perceptible chill I felt, sweat escaped my brow in a trickle and I prayed to my mother that Gjalpa not notice my discomfort.

Finally, the clang releasing us from our lessons sounded. Better to have poisonous venom dripped on my face for all eternity than to have to experience that awkwardness again. Gjalpa arose before the bell could finish chiming and quickly exited the class.

"Loki." It was Eilif, already at my side. These people moved quickly. "Wow, did you pierce Gjalpa's heart with a mistletoe arrow or what?"

"What?! Of—of course not, why would you ask such a thing? And with such a choice of weapon? I ... whatever do you mean?"

"Hey, take it easy," he said. "I've just never seen her act like that before, that's all."

So this was not her normal behavior. I carried home that small comfort.

The night was a long one for me. My dog had yet to be sent to me, and I missed his company. But I became even more dismayed when I replayed Gjalpa's bizarre behavior over and over in my head. She didn't know me well enough to behave in such a manner.

I was also troubled by the fact that this bothered me. I have e'er been alone but not lonely. Until now. Loki, the One, the ever-present, the independent trickster-god, could not escape the pangs of loneliness that washed over him. Er, me. The barn floor was especially uncomfortable this night, and sleep was long in coming.

The next day was better ... and worse. All night, I dreaded Gjalpa's angry glances to come the next day. I longed to confront her and demand to know what her problem was. It seemed somehow important to know.

It turned out that my sleepless night was for naught, as she wasn't in school at all. None of the Geirrods were. It was especially disheartening to realize this since the sun broke through a bit, making the day rather pleasant, for a land in the throes of a year-long third winter, that is.

Gjalpa and her adopted family didn't attend school the rest of the week.

The following week, walking across the meadow to my Armament class, I noticed the Geirrods gathered around the chariot parking area, feeding their horses. They joked and laughed with one another. In short, they looked like normal kids. Taller by far than the others, yes, but lighter of spirit than I saw upon my first introduction to them. I wondered if my great sense of loneliness was what caused me to project such strange personality traits on Gjalpa upon meeting her.

Gjalpa turned suddenly, again staring across the field and, seemingly, directly into my eyes.

Even worse, she suddenly began walking this way.

I hesitated for a moment, turning this way and that, pondering which way to go just long enough for her to appear in front of me, cutting off any escape option. Giantesses can cover a lot of ground very quickly, I noted mentally.

"Hello," she said. Her voice was like the beating of a snow owl's wings across a crisp winter's night. Unsure of myself in her presence, I said nothing.

"Hello," she repeated, not acknowledging my awkwardness. "My name is Gjalpa Geirrod. I didn't have a chance to introduce myself before. You must be ... Loki."

"H-how do you know my name? I mean, why did you call me Loki?"

"Well, in class when you sat by me, the professor called you that name. "

"Ahh, right. That vile, disgusting dwarf."

She smiled. "Yes, the teacher. You raised your hand when he referred to you as 'Loki,' so it seemed reasonable to assume that that was indeed your name."

"In-indeed." Stupid stupid stupid. I brought my gaze up to her face, an action which required me to crane my neck nearly to its breaking point. It was then I noticed her eyes.

"Did you ... did you go sleepless last night?" As soon as I asked the question, I regretted it. Stupid stupid stupid.

"No," she said. Her eyes were blazing red right now, a contrast to the deep black the first day I saw her. I noticed she clenched her hand into a fist again. But despite that implied threat of violence upon my person, or perhaps because of it, I felt a sense of calm around Gjalpa. Calm like I had rarely known in all my days.

We spoke not again of her changing eye color—really, for one such as I who could alter his physical appearance into any living creature, what difference did variable eye color make? Our conversation continued on.

"It's good news about the snow, isn't it?"

"Not really," I said.

"You don't like the cold? You'd think that nearly a full calendar's turn of the same weather might have acclimated you."

"It's ... not my favorite," I said. I wanted to be more forthcoming with this person. I wanted to tell her how I felt a connection with her already, but I dared not say more. Yet.

"Perhaps the amassing fire demons will bring a more temperate clime," she said. I only think she was joking. "You must find Jotunheim a difficult place to live."

"You have no idea. However, an unpleasant life is still preferable to the alternative back home. Things there were ... complicated."

"Why did you come here? You can tell me."

"I ..." I hesitated. Were my secret to get out, the rending of my limbs could be soon to follow. And I was rather attached to my limbs, and they to me. However, there was something in her plaintive manner that appealed to me. I let down my guard and told her who I was. I told her everything. Only later would I realize what a mistake this was.

"... and so, it was really nothing more than a prank gone wrong. Grear Balder used to boast of his impervious nature, how only the mistletoe plant could gravely harm him. Am I truly to be faulted for putting that boast to the test? Yes, Balder was the most beloved of all the northern gods, and yes, he was slain by a mistletoe arrow that did indeed pierce his heart. Some could argue that I was directly responsible for this death."

"*Some?*" She smiled again, eyes blazing red but possessing no judgment in them.

"Okay, well, *all.* But really, he must share some blame for making that kind of boast. It felt like a direct challenge to one such as me."

Was I saying too much? I kept the story as truthful as possible, although I did not mention the fact that I would indeed have slain that preening fool myself had I thought I could get away with it. Instead, I armed the blind god Höðr with an arrow carved from mistletoe. But how could I have known that the unseeing fool would strike a killing blow?

"The one thing I hear of mistletoe," she said smiling, "is that the plant has other, more ... mutually *beneficial* ... uses than just mayhem."

And with that, Loki's own heart suddenly felt pierced. We spoke no more. She looked down into my eyes. I stared up at her, her head looming large in my vision, a source of brightness amidst the storm clouds that had again gathered overhead.

I know not how long we spoke, for time stopped moving during our conversation. However, when it did restart, it did so in a hurry. As we stood in the field, a carriage led by two large horses started to take flight in the distance behind us. But as I would learn later, the foolish coachmen only had with him one large carrot, and neither horse was willing to share with the other. The piebald horse slammed his head into the other horse in an attempt to snatch the carrot away. This sent the carriage careening wildly out of control. Right for us!

The coachman was helpless to stop this as the horses battled, themselves oblivious to anyone in their path. The carriage slid recklessly out of control across the ground, with us in its path. As much as the fates like to predict our end, they are often wrong, and I assumed that my time of demise was only seconds away.

Suddenly, Gjalpa leapt in front of me, crouching down and touching the ground with both hands, palms pressed flat against the hard-packed dirt.

The horses and the carriage suddenly slid to either side of us, as though they struck patches of ice that did not exist moments before. The carriage slammed hard into the wall to the left of us, although I did not see this—I had shut tight my eyes, preparing for the crushing impact.

I opened my eyes and saw Gjalpa looking into them. The redness I saw in her eyes before was gone, her eyes again beautiful black pools. "Loki—Loki, are you all right?!"

"I-I'm fine," I said. I cast my eyes to the carriage. The horses were damaged, perhaps unable to ever fly again, but still living. The coachman was less fortunate. Which mattered not, since had he not perished in this collision, he would have met Loki later this evening and learned a valuable—and final—lesson in driving care. As it was, I made a mental note to revisit the two horses at midnight and impart the same lesson. My puppy, being sent to me this afternoon, would be in need of a good snack.

"Gjalpa, how ... how did you turn the carriage so? It appeared to strike twin patches of ice, but the ground...."

"The ground on which we stand has no such ice, Loki. I was right next to you. The horses luckily veered off at the last instant."

As she helped me off the ground, I doubted my senses, and I doubted her story more. Magic was not exactly an unknown commodity in my life, and I was sure

I saw something magical today. "No, you were ... in front of me. But you touched the ground, and then they slid away...."

"No, no."

"Yes, I saw you, Gjalpa."

"No. Please, Loki, *trust me.*"

I wanted to trust her. I did. But fooling the eyes of a trickster-god is easier said than done. Still, I felt a bond with her that was new and surprising to me, and not so easily discarded. So I chose not to press the issue. The important fact of the situation—that Loki yet lived—was the only tangibly important detail anyway, and so I let the matter drop.

"I—thank you, Gjalpa. For, um, talking to me, I mean. I am—I should go. I'm a bit shaken up, and I must prepare my barn for the arrival of my dog. He is being sent to me, and he'll be hungry. I must prepare for him a nice *supper.*" I looked at the two injured horses as I said this.

We parted. She went back to rejoin her adopted family, and the crowd that had gathered similarly departed. No one wanted to be present when the foolish coachman was spirited away to the halls of the dead lest his guides decide he needed additional company on that particular journey.

Yet I stayed. I bent down to touch the ground in front of me. While all the hard-packed soil was cold to the touch—nothing in this endless winter town was anything but cold—I could have sworn that I felt icy patches that dissipated under the warmth of my touch. Nothing was visible to the eye, and so I had no proof.

I considered what this meant, and tried to make sense of the jumbled thoughts running around through my head. I felt like I was close to puzzling out what I was thinking, for I felt a familiarity with Gjalpa, a kinship unlike any I'd known before. I might well have avoided the anguish to come had I not been interrupted, but a crackling in the sky jolted me from my reverie.

2. THIRD WHEEL

I'd been told many things about the Valkyries from my father and the elder gods. Those death-obsessed riders of winged horses, those shield-maiden choosers of the slain, those vengeful spirit-warriors who would not only take departed souls to the death-land of Valhalla but also, occasionally and capriciously, grab those still living and take them there as well. These horrid creatures were said to be monstrous in appearance, horrible of manner and blackened of soul.

"You only ever want to meet the Valkyries *once* in your life," my father told me as a child. "And even then, many souls wither in their presence before ever being able to complete the journey to Valhalla's fabled halls."

It seems my father never met hyperbole he didn't love. For the Valkyries who appeared now in front of me through an electrified hole in the sky possessed one other trait my father neglected to mention, or perhaps never knew for himself (after all, with only one eye, it's difficult to see things clearly)—they were impossibly, inarguably gorgeous.

As the three riders entered the school grounds on winged horses so white in color that they fairly glowed with brilliant light, the shield-maidens themselves nearly burned my eyes, so great was their beauty.

One in particular especially caught my eye. Never before today had the eyes of Loki been so ensnared so easily, but for the second time in recent memory, I was seized by feelings new and unexplored.

The third Valkyrie to exit the rift in the air was also the youngest. She appeared roughly my age, while the other two were visibly older and battle-hardened.

The other two administered to the needs of the deceased coachmen, but the smaller one approached me. "Who are you, o man, that you stand in the presence of the Valkyries with gaze that withers not?"

Formal types, these Valkyries. "I am Loki," I said.

"Brynhilda, I," she said. Her hair was the finest gold, woven into lustrous, thick braids. Her silver battle armor seemed to be protecting a very pleasant figure.

"And who are ... you know, your friends?"

"Friends we are not, godling. We are Valkyries one and all. My companions Geirdriful and Geiravör are both known for their prowess with the spear, as well as their caring touch in bringing the einherjar to Valhalla's hallowed halls."

"'Einherjar'? Surely a reckless fool who ran himself into a wall, nearly striking my person while doing so, doesn't qualify as a valiant warrior worthy of Valhalla?"

As Brynhilda started to answer, her shrewish companions cast their gaze in our direction. "Brynhilda! Leave the mortal alone and help us administer to this dead soul!"

She scoffed in their general direction. "Surely two such capable Valkyries as you are capable of preparing one mortal without young Brynhilda getting in your way!"

I whispered to her, suppressing my smile at her sharp tongue. "Can you also tell them that Loki is no mortal but a god most strong?"

They shouted back at her. "Foolish girl! Dost you not know that you talk to Loki the viper, Loki the snake, Loki the Balder-killer?"

Such was my lot when my reputation preceded me. There was no hiding anything from Valkyries.

"That was *you*?!" Brynhilda smiled largely enough to reveal to me all of her perfect teeth. "Pay them no mind, Loki Odinson! Valhalla's halls are better for having the great Balder in it. And to have orchestrated the death of one so fair and beloved, heedless of the consequences to come, well, that is ... that's just *cool!*"

Her stoic Valkyrie demeanor disappeared and she was a girl again. A girl with a battle-sharpened sword and fitted armor of the finest metals, but a girl in Loki's presence nonetheless. It appeared that even Valkyries who whiled away their days taking away departed warriors preferred the company of "bad boy" gods like myself. Would that I had known before that my machinations would prove so appealing to the fair sex.

"Fair Brynhilda, when you mentioned before that my actions against Balder had great consequences, what did you mean?"

"Oh, never mind that now, Loki. Come, let us take a flight and talk a while." She reached down from her perch upon her steed, offering her hand so that I might join her on the back of her horse. Only, her horse was having none of that. Flaring flames from its nostrils, the horrid creature whipped its head around at me and would have snapped my hand off in its powerful jaws had Brynhilda not intervened. "Er, that is, come, Loki, let us instead take a walk. My horse will wait here for us."

It appears none but Valkyries may sit upon their horses. Which suited me just fine. Perhaps my fair pup could use a meal of *three* such animals tonight, instead of just the two I already planned....

Upset were Brynhilda's traveling companions, but even they admitted that the wretch they were carting away did not require the aid of three Valkyries. They allowed her pass, commenting that they appreciated the constant business I sent their way, and also looked forward to seeing me very soon. Which sounded on the surface to be a polite thing to say, but their wicked smiles told me there was deeper and more disconcerting meaning behind their words.

At the moment, I cared not about such things. I was entranced by Brynhilda as we walked. Partly because she seemed entranced with me, and any girl who admired Loki deserved in turn my admiration for their strikingly good taste.

"That coachman your Valkyrie-sisters spirited away—why did he gain admittance to a hall of warriors, anyway? Have the qualifications for Valhalla lapsed?"

Brynhilda, who also stood nearly a head's length taller than me, considered this even as she used her sword as a walking stick, absentmindedly carving lines in the ground with its tip as we walked. "No. He was, as you say, a fool. But the coming conflagration—an event that will be forever marked as starting with your plot against fair Balder—will fill Valhalla's halls with warriors, and our need for servants to suit their needs has grown."

"*My* actions, you say?"

"Why, yes, Loki. Twilight is approaching. Fair Balder's passing has ignited the flames of war, and the fire-demons from the depths have amassed an army of considerable enough size to finally—"

I cut her off with another question. "Never mind that now," I said. "Since you Valkyries seem to know so much about, well, everything, what do you know of the Geirrods? Are they normal?"

"The Geirrods? The girl who helped the demise of yon coachmen? The other shield-maidens said that she is one of the cold ones."

"The cold ones?"

She stopped and looked directly into my eyes. "Yes. The Jotun. Your people call them *frost giants*. According to legend," she continued, noting the shock in my eyes, "they are the bane of the gods and the natural enemy of us Valkyries."

"But ... why? They seem ... well, they seem nice."

"Nice they are not, Loki. For, you see, their abilities are not only far beyond those of mortals, but their way of dealing with threats benefits not Valhalla. They tend to freeze their enemies, encasing them in glacier-thick blocks. This leaves them incapacitated, forever removed from the field of battle, but still living. And as such, off-limits to us Valkyries and denied rightful admittance to Valhalla."

"But," I countered, "if they are not claiming the lives of warriors, this makes them not dangerous to be around, right? These Geirrods, they're not like the frost giants of eons past, are they?"

"No," she said, getting gravely serious. "They're not *like* those horrible frost giants from days of yore."

"They are the *same* ones."

My slumber that evening was again long in coming. Brynhilda eventually took her leave, returning to Valhalla in an acrid burst of smoke and lightning. She told me she would have difficulty returning to see me without just cause, said cause being another dead soul to cart away to the great hall. I told her that I could see to that on a regular enough basis should she decide that she would like to see me again. She said she would, and she leaned in and kissed me on the cheek, sending a jolt of electricity through me.

I instantly began plotting out who I could trick into dying so that I might see her again.

At school the next day, I made it through the rest of my studies in a daze. In part because there was nothing to be learned about life from repulsive dwarves and the other moronic persons presented to me as educators. Better that Loki should educate them about the ways of the world by cleaving their heads from their shoulders. But I digress.

I had much to ponder. Loki the loveless, Loki the forlorn, Loki the ever-detested ... this is who I was in Asgard. This is how I saw myself. And suddenly, to be given a different perspective twice in the course of one day was worth heavy consideration.

I did feel a kinship with Gjalpa that was hard to explain, although made easier by the suggestion of her origin, considering the rumors of my own frost-giant lineage.

Then again, perhaps the frost-giant rumor was just Brynhilda looking to undercut the competition. After all, if she knew upon arrival that I was the Loki who was responsible for filling her hall with saps like Balder, then could she not also peer into my heart and see that I was smitten with Gjalpa?

Similarly, did Brynhilda realize that her very nature drew me to her as well? A shield maiden who proved to be so much more alluring than I was ever led to believe was an intriguing prospect indeed.

Was this what it had come to so suddenly? Choosing between Team Gjalpa or Team Brynhilda?

Perhaps I could seek to date both of these enchanting creatures? After all, was I not Loki, the great trickster? If I could not maintain the deception of becoming embroiled in relationships with both of these delights, was I any more worthy of my nickname than Eilif was of his?

I feel that loyalty is for lesser men. Or for bramble-headed louts like my half-brother Thor, who had not the brainpower to consider loving more than one other at a time. But I was not cut from that same simple sackcloth. Rather, if gods like my own father Odin had shown me anything, it was that all options are viable, and all outlets are to be pursued simultaneously. Great Loki the unloved deserved to make up for lost time. And besides, if Brynhilda could only come see me while also collecting the dead, I could just schedule those visits carefully around any other engagements I might have. *This could work.*

But first, the question of Gjalpa's origin needed to be answered.

It was yet another dreary, cloudy day, the air growing ever more frigid. Fimbul Winter was seriously unpleasant the longer it persisted. Had I been informed that my machinations against Balder would result in such a terrible climate, I might well have chosen another god against whom to focus my ire.

I saw Surty upon arriving on the school grounds. She was speaking conspiratorially with two other fire demons, neither of whom were familiar to me.

"Good morn to you, Loki. Enjoying the cold weather? For now?" She winked at the other two.

"Yes, well, a good morning would be one that does not freeze the air in my lungs, Surty," I said. The two fire demons with her chuckled at that, though I knew not why.

"Coming right up," she said. Again, the other two laughed. I kept walking, paying no heed to that foolish girl or her flaming compatriots. In another day, I might well have set rock vipers against their flaming ankles as payment for their folly, but today, I was too anticipatory over the idea of seeing Gjalpa again and had no time to listen to their prattling.

I saw her standing with her other "family" members, and once again, she seemed preternaturally aware of my presence and turned to look at me. Only this time, her eyes blazed and I could read them clearly, even from a distance: "Stay away."

This girl was demonstrating considerable mastery at sending mixed signals. But I acquiesced, and went to class.

She took her seat next to me some time after the lessons had started. Her eyes were the color of deepest black.

"Gjalpa, I…."

"Shh, Loki. Not here."

"Not here? But we only sit and listen to a detestable dwarf. I will never take lessons from such a monster, I will—"

"Loki, *please*. I know you have questions."

How could she know that?

"After school. Meet me under the branches of Yggdrasil."

"Er, Gjalpa, if you're not aware, the great world-tree's branches extend out across the nine realms. One could spend several lifetimes searching under those limbs and never find what he was looking for."

"Silly. Under the *big* branch, I mean. The one that blocks all of the sun's rays from reaching Jotunheim."

Silly. She called me silly. Whereas before, Loki would have plucked out the tongue of any who dared refer to me in such a way, when she said it, it made me warm inside. And in this terrible winter-world in which we all now lived, I would take the warmth where it came. *Silly*. This girl was utterly charming.

If she told me then that she possessed the power to read minds, I would not have doubted it, for she suddenly turned and looked at me with a smile that set my heart soaring into Yggdrasil's great branches already.

After our lessons were complete—lessons that had me plotting out the demise of someone who would allow me to see Brynhilda soon (the dwarf was my leading candidate)—I briskly made my way to great Yggdrasil.

It is difficult for the mortal mind to fathom Yggdrasil's size. Its mammoth trunk out of which its world-encompassing branches grew was thick enough at the base to require seven lifetimes to walk a circle around it. Its branches spanned galaxies, extending across all horizons of possibilities. But even amongst that unfathomable largeness, there was one limb that stood out. Fortunately, its location was near enough to Jotunheim that I reached it in a reasonable amount of time. Under this branch, the sun has never shown through—not even a sliver of its rays could penetrate the canopy above. It was there that I waited for Gjalpa. I did not have to wait long.

"I'm sorry about earlier today," she said upon arrival, her appearance next to me surprising me despite the fact that I was always at the ready for anything. Her speed belied her size. "My ... brothers and sisters, they are wary of me getting too close to outsiders."

"Outsiders? Then let me *in*, Gjalpa. I have no wish to remain on the outside. I feel ... a connection with you. A closeness I wish to nurture. I just ... I need to know some things before I can fully surrender to the feelings I have now."

"Loki, these words you tell me, they should scare me away. I am not so quickly drawn to others. I don't easily let down my guard, but something about you ... it makes me think that I could see myself spending all day with you. Every day."

All day? *Every* day? "Gjalpa, I-I think I know why your eye color changes as it does."

"Oh, is that so," she said, arching an eyebrow under which sat an ebony eyeball.

"Yes, when I first saw you, your eyes were black as a dwarf's heart, curse that hated race. But then, another time, they flamed red."

"Is my eye color really what you have questions about, gentle Loki?"

Gentle? Me?

"In truth, Gjalpa, no. It was ... when the carriage nearly struck me, it slid out of the way on patches of ice. Patches *you* created."

She dropped her eyes. But was that still a small smile pursing her lips? "This, again? How would I even do something like that, Loki? I am no goddess of the type you knew back in Asgard. I am a simple, humble—"

"—frost giantess," I finished.

She looked up at me. "Oh, that is ... what—why would you say such a thing?"

"It makes sense, Gjalpa. The ice patches. Your immense size. Your eye color changing from black to red when your temperature warms. Besides, I was talking to the Valkyrie and she said—"

"*Which* Valkyrie? When were you talking to a Valkyrie? And *why*?" She demanded, eyes blazing cold black fire. I saw her hands ball up into fists, and this time, so tight did she clench that particles of ice formed on the outside of her knuckles.

"Um, yesterday, when they collected the body, I stayed and talked to one of them, Brynhilda. She was ... she was nice." I said that last part in barely more than a whisper.

"*Nice*?! Valkyries are not nice! They steal the souls from men, which they then trap inside a placid hall, far away from the battlefield! That is torture for warriors born! And it seems they also use their evil ways to spread foul and deceitful rumors about others."

Now, typically, when I have had conversations with women about affairs of the heart, it has ended with me either deceiving them into making a decision that they ultimately regret, or perhaps just transforming them into field mice to be eaten by crows. So my reaction to Gjalpa's anger was surprising to me. I reached for her hand.

My palm made contact with her knuckles and stuck, so icily dry was her hand, so teeth-chatteringly cold. But I didn't care.

"Gjalpa, fair Gjalpa. I know not the truth of my own origins; I only know the rumors and hearsay that the children of Asgard whisper about me. So I am not one to sit in judgment over another in this regard. Besides, I have only heard tell of how proud are the frost giants. They battle against the gods, knowing full well that the gods are more powerful but never acquiescing. Why, my own doltish brother alone has slain many a frost gi— er, I mean, they have my respect. As would you. If that was indeed your true nature."

"My true nature, as you put it, Loki, necessitates that I hide who I am. It's not so easy. Why do you think I am absent on some days?"

"I ... I only know that on those days, my heart feels diminished."

She smiled a sad smile at me, and then stood, drawing herself up to her full, considerable height.

"Then perhaps I should demonstrate what would happen were I to show up at school on days when the sun does break through. Loki, if you will. The great limb of the world-tree that blots out the sun over Jotunheim—pull it back that the sun's rays might finally peek through. Even in this Fimbul Winter, it's a rather temperate day, and the sun will be eager to break through a spot it has never had a chance to caress before."

I did as she asked. I quickly wove a lasso out of discarded leaves and branches and, turning into an eagle to allow me to fly it up high, circled the branch. We gods have tricks that mortals cannot even guess. I returned to my human form and pulled the loop taught, and yanked. The great limb creaked and groaned, but could not deny my godly power (well, once Gjalpa added her own considerable strength to the pulling, that is).

The branch bent and bowed downward, opening a hole in the canopy. Above it, the sun, so eager to reach this virgin spot of land upon which it had never been, cast sunny rays of warmth down, down.

The solar rays caressed Gjalpa. They didn't touch me, for Loki ever dwells in the shadows, but they did embrace the girl next to me, anyway. Her eyes softened and again changed from deepest black to darkest red. But even more surprising was the effect it had on her skin.

Her face and hands began to appear luminescent, sparkling as though her body were covered with thousands of tiny diamonds. Her skin's brilliance was stunning to behold. I was awestruck. Never have I seen a more beautiful, captivating sight. Her sparkling, bejeweled skin cast a glow of utter brilliance across the forest floor.

I was so taken aback by this that I saw great teardrops fall from my eyes and land at my feet. Only, it was then that I noticed that my eyes were in fact dry, and the falling drops of dew were coming from fair Gjalpa herself. Tears of her own? No—the drops were emitting from her cheeks, from her hands and wrists, her very fingertips seeming to melt, turning first to slush and then quickly to water.

"Um, Loki ... the branch—"

"Ahh! Right away, my sweet." We released the rope, the great branch snapping back into place, the sun once again denied access to this land.

Her skin quickly returned to its normal icy appearance. It was perhaps fortuitous that I brought on Fimbul Winter since, other than the fact that it is said to be the precursor to the gods' demise, its frigid temperatures quickly restored her to normal.

We sat under the branch a while, her hands in mine. "So, a little sunlight…."

"You see our dilemma. We quickly go from sparkling like jewels to puddling like dew drops. But Loki, thanks to you, and this tree, the sun need never reach me now. You give me hope of a shared existence. We could travel beyond the frigid wastelands of my homeland and see all there is to see. Every day, we could be together!"

"Every day? Well, now, see, Gjalpa, I do crave the idea of sharing my time with another, but maybe not *all* my time, if that makes any sense? I have much that I do, and some of that time requires it be spent away from the accompaniment of others."

She placed her other hand on top of mine. And squeezed. I could feel my very marrow drop by degrees as she did so.

"Now, Loki, it is not the way of the frost giant to have dalliances. We keep to our own kind out of an effort to protect one another from hostiles. So the only way for me to bring an outsider—especially a god who has admitted his own brother has slain my kind—is for us to form an ever-lasting and impenetrable bond with one another. This is what I require of you, Loki. This is what must be, if *we* are to be."

I did my best to mask the look of growing horror in my eyes. Spend every minute with another, even someone I had started to care about? Be showered with affection all day long, without end? How could anyone of independent mind and means truly want such a thing?

I was quickly leaning toward Team Brynhilda, when all of a sudden, the branches suddenly exploded around us. Fragments of wood and leaf peppered across our faces and arms. I was momentarily blinded by the maelstrom, but unfortunately, my other senses were not similarly dulled. My nose still worked, and it detected a familiar scent of electricity. Brynhilda was *here*.

She flew into the clearing, leaping from her steed before it had even set foot on the ground. She drew her sword and walked toward us, her heavy bootfalls making deep impressions in the soft ground. The swaying of her sword back and forth made a deep impression upon me.

"Loki! What is the meaning of this? What are you doing here with ... *her*?!"

"Er, hello, Brynhilda. Who died and made you, uh, work?"

"Never mind that! Well, if you must know, an oafish Valhallain exchange student named Eilif got himself lost and ended up getting the other half of his face burned off in an Advanced Smelting class. That drew me back to Jotunheim, only to find you absent from school and cavorting under Yggdrasil's fair branches with a lowly *frost giant*!"

"Eilif? Poor Eilif met an untoward end again?"

"Loki, what does that bovine mean, 'lowly frost giant'?!"

"Loki! What does *she* mean by 'bovine'?!"

Things were quickly spiraling out of control. I had to get control over this situation before things became so untenable as to alert Heimdall or the other Asgardians as to my location. As it was, entirely too many people in Jotunheim had learned my true nature.

"Girls! Can we all just calm down—and keep our voices down? There is no need for such enmity."

They both turned as one and glared at me, cowing me into silence, until I thought of what Brynhilda had said.

"Did you, fair Brynhilda, really say that the name of the recent departed was Eilif?"

"I did. His dwarvish teacher miscalculated a lesson and Eilif suffered as a result. But his suffering is like nothing compared to the suffering you will undergo, should you choose the company of that vile frost giant over that of my own."

Well, now I had even more reason to escape this predicament, so I might pay back that horrible dwarf for his folly. It seemed my dog would soon eat well all week, assuming I was still mobile and had all limbs attached with which to feed him.

"We were ... just talking, Brynhilda," I started.

"Just talking! Loki, you were professing your undying love to me," said Gjalpa, ruining the moment I was trying to create.

"Undying, eh? We shall see about that!" And with that, Brynhilda reached down with one hand and plucked me from where I stood, throwing me into the clearing and advancing on me. She poked her sword into the underside of my jaw, and we were suddenly full circle with where this tale began.

"Loki, before I separate your lying head from your bony shoulders, I give you one more chance—be true to your word and offer *me* your heart forever, that you may accompany me on my tasks and serve my needs. I am a Valkyrie and cannot shirk my duties, so this is what is required that we might be together."

Well. That didn't sound much fun at all. Suddenly, the option of her removing my head from its shoulders didn't sound like the worst option presented before me.

Brynhilda's blade was knocked away by a ball of ice. It was followed quickly by two more ice-balls, hurled at great velocity by Gjalpa.

"Hands off, shield-witch! Loki is *mine!*"

Brynhilda blocked the second ball of ice with her metal wrist guards, but the first struck her squarely in the face. She spit out ice and epithets with equal rancor. "Foul, frigid snow-pig! Loki is *mine*, heart and soul! Especially soul! You cold-hearted monsters don't know the first thing about how to properly love another!"

"Oh, but I suppose *you* do, you carrion-carrier!"

This was getting interesting. Gjalpa ran forward and grappled with Brynhilda, knocking her sword from her grasp. It landed near my feet. As the fighting devolved into thuggery, I rapidly weighed my options.

Clearly, the idea of dating both women would avail me not. And after hearing the words that came out of both mouths during the heated arguing, it had me suddenly wondering if I should instead remain a solo player. Perhaps Team Loki had no room for such controlling types after all. Loneliness was a state with which I was well accustomed, and it was obvious that I would not willingly give up my independence in trade for fealty and servitude. My heart, which had always operated independently of others, had tricked me into thinking it needed companionship.

Trickery. Of course. Was I not, despite my recent foray into romantic ineptitude, still Loki? A solution—the only true solution—presented itself to me.

I picked up Brynhilda's sword (only with great effort. I managed to choose two of the strongest women I have ever come in contact with, another good reminder that I would be wise to find my way out of this double-sided predicament).

As my two potential consorts fought on, I swung her sword around twice, spinning my body to build up momentum. I then released the blade upward with all my might. The sword spun end over end into the sky, finally striking the great branch I had earlier pulled back. The sword's honed edge cleaved through the giant limb without effort. The branch, separated from the trunk, started to move and sway. Finally, the weight of it pulled it loose, and the great branch fell.

It plunged down, down, and the whistling sound of its descent was great enough to stop the two warrior-women from the battles.

"Loki—" they said in unison, but only one of the two uttered my name with any confidence.

As the branch traveled downward, so too did the sun's rays. Once again they bathed Gjalpa, and Brynhilda as well. Frankly, the two women looked utterly gorgeous inside the funnel of warm light.

Then Gjalpa's skin took on its bejeweled tone again, although it began melting at the same time. The concentration of the sun's rays, with no canopy with which to slow it, accelerated its effect on her. And this time, there *were* tears intermingling with the drops of water emitting from her skin—both hers and mine.

As Gjalpa began puddling across the forest floor, she looked at me for the last time. Her legs had melted away enough that she was now my height and looking me directly in the eyes for a moment, before continuing her moist downward trajectory.

"I am undone, Loki," she gurgled, "may you forever burn in fiiiiiiiire...." She trailed off. Liquefied lips can't easily utter words, it seems.

I felt a tinge of sadness, but fought it off when I reminded myself that Loki was never meant to be simple husband to anyone. Now, on to the second part of my quickly thrown-together scheme. I spun around to look at the Valkyrie.

Brynhilda was grinning from ear to ear. She pulled loose her sword, which had also fallen back to earth and embedded itself up to its hilt, and stepped toward me.

"Loki! I knew from the moment I met you that you had sharp senses! You knew that frigid behemoth wasn't right for you, and you knew I was! Oh, Loki!"

She rushed toward me, planning to embrace me. I grasped her shoulders and held her away, at arm's length. "Aren't you forgetting something, fair Valkyrie?" I motioned to the puddle on the ground.

"Oh, I will never forget what you have done! You have chosen a life with me, my lord. We should get to work at once, making plans and sharing our lives!"

"Well, one of us should get to work anyway, only it is not wise Loki."

"What are you—" The reality of the situation began to settle in, if the look in her eyes was any indication.

"You, my Brynhilda, are a *Valkyrie*. While a life of acquiescing to your demands and carrying your helmet while you work might hold appeal to some, it holds absolutely none for Loki. But my lack of interest in your profession does not negate the fact that you are required to see those labors through now."

As I spoke, Gjalpa's spirit arose from the moist ground. "The giantess perished in battle, and is awaiting its final ride to Valhalla's halls. You cannot deny your responsibilities, Brynhilda. You are a Valkyrie first, as you reminded me. Gjalpa has earned her seat inside the hall. Best be off with you, then, before your maiden-sisters become aware of you shirking your duties. I do not imagine that would sit well."

She stared at me with death in her eyes. But maybe it was just a trick of the light. No, it was probably death. Pulling her sword and waving it in my direction, she screamed, "Perhaps I should take *two* recently departed souls with me to Valhalla, deceitful snake!"

"Ahh, Brynhilda," I sighed, picking an errant branch shard out of my teeth. "Would that the Valkyries were understanding enough for you to set aside responsibilities in order to carry out your petty grievances and keep poor, departed souls waiting. But I do not believe they are. Best be off now. Alas, our love just cannot work around such requirements. Would that it were not so."

I turned away, lest my growing smile turn into outright laughter. She knew she had no recourse. To betray the trusted duties of a Valkyrie was to renounce one's heritage and be kicked out of Valhalla for all time. I was counting on her hate for me not being quite great enough to supercede her desire to remain within those hallowed halls. I was right, but barely.

As Brynhilda saw to her labors, I looked at the two one last time. Gjalpa's shade was now in the Valkyrie's grasp and being prepared for her trip to Valhalla. If looks could kill, well, my own twilight would be upon me sooner than was written.

"Farewell, my ladies fair. Would that things could have been different. But, as the expression goes, Loki dost not need any clinging vines. Farewell."

"Loki," I heard Brynhilda say. I looked at her. Gjalpa's soul sat perched on the winged horse behind Bryn. She refused to turn her head toward me. But Brynhilda did, and her eyes blazed with red-hot anger so great that I wondered if she too was part frost giant. "The Twilight of the Gods is upon the land. Your death is foretold, and is imminent. So don't think we will be separated for long. For when your corpse settles onto the ground during the coming battle, I will be there personally to see that you are taken to Valhalla, where we may spend all eternity together."

"And Loki," she paused. "Once inside the great hall, the only kisses I plan to shower you with shall be made of tempered steel."

She dug her heels into her horse, and the beast at once began flapping its great wings, until she and Gjalpa rose off into the sky and out of sight.

Again with this talk about a coming battle and Loki's imminent demise. My current dating situation resolved, it was now time I did something about that as well.

3. MATCH-MAKING

As I exited the forest and was free of Yggdrasil's shade, I noticed that the problem with the cloudy and frozen sky had begun to resolve itself, in the form of great flames that licked across the horizon. It seems that our Twilight was upon us. The gods were destined to fall.

On the long and thankfully lonely walk out of the forest, I began thinking about the various things people had said when speaking of the coming battle. Surty and her flame-demon friends had definitely talked about things I chose not to hear because I was too taken with affairs of the heart. Which was yet another reason to remain so unencumbered. One can only properly see to one's own survival without the blinders of love.

The gist of what everyone said about the imminent end of everything is that it all began with Balder's death. Would that I had known ... well, I would not have changed a thing. That prig needed to be taken down. But this meant that if I was responsible for starting this process, I should similarly be able to stop it, at least where my own personal doom was concerned. All of Asgard could go hang for all I cared. If enabling Balder to die also helped bring about the doom of Thor, Heimdall and the others, well, that was a better chain reaction than I could have hoped. But the loss of Loki would be too great indeed, at least to me. Still, we all had a part to play, and I would play mine. At least to a point.

It was not fated that Loki would meet his end during our coming Twilight—it was *written*. That makes a world of difference. The Fates are rarely wrong about their castings, but the men who write things down and pass them off as fact are prone to mortal error.

As I returned home and found my dog at last waiting for me, I thought about the end of the gods. Many of them deserved to fade away into the twilight, or to be locked away in Valhalla's musty halls. After all, the gods as I knew them were capricious creatures, driven as much by emotion and lust as by reason and need. But I, up until my most recent escapade, was not. I was and am fueled by a much stronger thing—the desire to make mischief and to do wrong unto others. And it was precisely those things that made me realize I needed to live beyond our foretold ending. Loki is necessary in the world to come, whereas the other gods are not.

"Here, pup! Here, boy!" My beloved pooch ran to me, licking hunger across his lips.

"Good boy! Are you hungry, pup? Well, let us be off, then, my little *Fenris*. It's finally time for you to sup. I spotted a full moon peeking out from behind a cloud on my walk back here. Perhaps that planetoid would make a good first morsel for you. But save a bit of room, for I've a nice dwarf-snack in mind for you, too."

As my dog, Fenris the Wolf, leapt into the heavens, prepared to devour sun, moon, and gods alike, I wondered what the fire-demoness Surty was doing right now. It occurred to me that I should call on her. Her team was leading the charge against the gods and she was positioned to know victory in the coming battle. Plus, she was cute enough. She could likely use a good consort to accompany her through.

And if that potentially star-crossed romance didn't survive the terrible battle to come, perhaps upon my return in the next world, I should try my luck dating a vampire. I heard they are rather easy to manipulate.

Vicious

By

Mark Morris

There was this bird. John said she was bad news. But then John thinks everyone's bad news. He's just fucking paranoid.

Not as bad as Malcolm, though. Malcolm thinks the CIA and the FBI and fuck knows who else is following us. He thinks they're waiting for the chance to blow us all away. Wipe the Sex Pistols off the face of the earth.

Well, ha fucking ha. They won't get me. I'm Sid Vicious. I'm fucking indestructible. I'm gonna live forever.

This bird, though. Came on to me after the gig. These American birds love me. "Sid, Sid, fuck me." "Yeah, alright, darlin'. Anything to oblige."

John says I'm disgusting. He says I'm turning into a Rolling Stone. But he's just uptight and jealous. He ain't as pretty as me. Ain't got no anarchy in his soul no more. I'm the only one with any anarchy left. Steve and Paul. What a couple of cunts. They're just the backing band. After the gig tonight Steve went mental. Said I was out of control. Said I was dragging them all down.

"We're *supposed* to be out of control, you fucker," I told him. "We're the Sex Pistols."

He told me if I didn't sort myself out I'd be out of the band.

"You can't throw me out," I said. "You'd be nothing without me. People don't come to see you. They come to see me."

"Yeah," said John. He was sitting in the corner on his own, with a can of beer in his hand like an old man in a pub. "But that's 'cos most of the morons who go to the circus prefer the clowns to the artistes."

He don't know what he's talking about. He's so full of shit. He's a miserable bastard. They're all miserable bastards. Not me, though. I'm having a great time. I ain't got no gear, and that's fucking killing me, but at least I'm making an effort.

Thing is, I hurt all over from not having any stuff, and I can't sleep, and every time I eat something I throw it back up. And I fucking itch. Itch, itch, itch. All over. My arm, where I cut myself, and my chest, where I carved Gimme A Fix (and I don't even remember doing that), and my fucking bollocks. My bollocks most of all.

I thought I had some disease. I thought I was dying. Our tour manager, Noel Monk. He's a fucking hippie, with a moustache like a fucking faggot cowboy, but he's all right.

"Noel," I said. "There's something wrong with me. I fucked some bitch before I come here and I fucking itch like crazy."

He laughed. "Don't worry, Sid. You got crabs, that's all," he said.

So yeah. I hurt and I itch and I'm sick and I need some stuff so bad and I'm missing Nancy, but that don't stop me enjoying myself. Fucking America. It's great.

So this bird. She come up and she wanted to fuck me. We were hanging out after the show. We're in this place. Baton Rouge. Louisiana. The Kingfish Club.

I was feeling all right. I was drinking peppermint schnapps 'cos it stops the hurting, and Noel had given me some of his valiums, and I was floating. Everything soft and mellow. And this bird said, "Sid, you're beautiful. I want to fuck you."

And so we fucked. Right there on the bar. Animal magnetism. People were watching and taking photos, but I didn't care. Let 'em. It's their problem if they wanna be perverts, not mine.

She was going down on me, and I was lying back, thinking of England (ha ha ha) and then there was all this shouting, and I opened my eyes, and there was Noel and Glen, one of the security blokes, and some other geezers, and everyone was going apeshit. Glen was trying to grab someone's camera and Noel was pulling the bird off me, and so I took a swing at him with my bottle, but I missed.

"What the fuck are you doing, Noel?" I said. "You said I could shag who I wanted."

It's true. He wouldn't get me no smack, but he said any time I saw a bird I liked he'd bring her to me.

"And so you can, Sid," he said. "But not here. Here is a bit too ... public."

I saw John out of the corner of my eye. He curled his lip and sneered at me. He looked disgusted.

"Where then?" I said.

"We'll find somewhere. Come on."

They took us away. Me and the bird. It was like being arrested. Surrounded by all these bodies. Big guys. Like a fucking moving wall. I saw faces through the wall. A blur of faces, looking at me. I spat at them. "Fuck off." They were like demons. Grinning. Eyes shining. "Fuck off, fuck off." I wanted to slash them all open.

We didn't have a hotel. When the equipment was packed we were all getting back on the bus and driving through the snow and the dark and the shit. Endless fucking black roads. Driving and driving.

I don't mind the driving, to be honest. It's a bit boring, but it's all right. I like that we stop at roadside diners. Steak and eggs. I love my steak and eggs. Steak rare, eggs runny. But I can never keep it down. Eat it all up, yum yum, lovely. But then my guts cramp and I have to run for the bog and throw it back up again. All over the wall. In the sink. Everywhere. Blood and puke all over America. Sid was here.

"Oi, Glen," I said.

Glen looked at me. He's a big fucking guy. Big fucking beard. I told him only hippies and arseholes have beards, but he's all right. Glen's tough.

"Yeah, Sid?"

"Where we going tonight?"

"When we've finished here, you mean?"

"Yeah."

"We're going to Dallas, Sid."

"Oh yeah," I said.

Dallas. That's where that President got shot. I remember my mum telling me about that when I was a kid. Big deal. Big news. Maybe we'll get shot in Dallas too. Maybe we'll be as famous as that President.

"Dallas," I said. "Yeah, brilliant."

Noel and Glen found us this place backstage. Fucking broom cupboard. Sink in the corner.

"We'll be right outside, Sid," Noel said, "so don't get any smart ideas about running out on us."

"I won't, Noel. No way."

He shut the door. It was fucking dark in there, but me and the bird fucked on the floor. I was knackered. I felt sick. I puked in the sink. My head was pounding.

"You okay, Sid?" the bird asked. She tried to touch me, but my skin was sore. Her touch was like needles. I shrugged her off.

"Don't fucking touch me," I said.

"Jeez," she said. "What's your problem?"

"You," I said. "You're my fucking problem."

She went all whiny. "What have I done wrong, Sid? Tell me what I've done wrong and I'll put it right."

"I need smack," I said. "You got any smack?"

"No," she said.

"Then you're no fucking good to me," I said. "Why don't you fuck off?"

She started to cry. Black lines trickling down her face. I felt bad. "Fucking hell," I said. "Don't cry."

"I can't help it. You're mad at me."

"No, I'm not," I said. "I'm not mad at you. I just need some stuff. Noel and that lot, they won't let me out. They won't let me go anywhere. They think if I go off somewhere I'll end up killing myself."

"And will you?" said the bird. Little squeaky voice.

I laughed. I was hurting again. Sweats and chills. Body cramps. "Yeah, probably," I said. "Or some fucking cowboy will shoot me. They hate us here. Fucking America hates the Sex Pistols."

"I don't," said the bird. "I love the Sex Pistols."

"Yeah, well, you're one of the smart ones," I said. "Most people are scared of us. They think we're gonna destroy America."

"You should," said the bird. "You should destroy America. It's a dump. I hate it."

"Yeah," I said. "It's a fucking dump."

"Maybe I'll come to England," the bird said.

"Don't bother," I said. "It's a dump there too."

I didn't wanna talk no more. I finished the Schnapps and curled up on the floor and closed my eyes. I hurt all over. I just wanted everything to go black.

"Do you want me to go?" the bird asked.

"I'm not bothered," I said. "Stay or go. I don't care."

I went to sleep. I had these dreams. Bad dreams. Faces looking at me. All these fucking faces. Shouting and laughing. Twisting out of shape. Turning into something bad. I was trying to push them away, but I was trapped. I couldn't get out. I couldn't breathe. I was a kid again. I was crying for my mum. I was cutting myself. Slash slash, across my arms, across my chest. I wanted the pain and the blood. But there was no pain, no blood. I couldn't make myself bleed. I couldn't feel anything. I cried out, but I couldn't make any noise.

"Shh, mon petit."

The voice was in my head. It went through me like a cold breeze on a hot day. It blew all the shit and fear away. Made me feel calm.

I opened my eyes. Big brown eyes looking down at me.

"Who are you?" I said.

This wasn't the bird I'd fucked earlier. This was someone different. Light brown skin. Smooth, like toffee. Big brown eyes and big red lips. Black hair in little twisty dreads. She was fucking beautiful. She was so beautiful I couldn't breathe.

"You want to be saved?" she said.

I was shivering. My leather jacket was over me like a blanket, but the floor was cold underneath me and I felt like there was nothing left of me but bones.

"Saved from what?" I said.

"From yourself."

"Dunno what you mean."

I tried to sit up. I felt so weak. She had to help me. She jangled when she moved. She was wearing all these bracelets and necklaces. She smelled like flowers and spice and dark forests.

"How did you get in here?" I asked her.

"I go where I please," she said.

She put her hand under the tap in the sink and turned it on. She held her dripping fingers over my face. I opened my mouth and the water ran over my lips and tongue and down my throat. It tasted sweet, made me feel like a kid again. Everything new and bright.

"You want to be saved?" she asked again.

I shrugged. "I dunno. Are you one of those Jesus nutjobs?"

She laughed. "I believe in spirits, mon petit. Do *you* believe in spirits?"

"Yeah," I said. "Whisky and vodka."

She didn't laugh this time. She reached out and touched a badge on my jacket. "Is this true?"

"What?"

"'I'm A Mess.' Is it true, mon petit? *Are* you a mess?"

I looked into her big brown eyes. They held me. They were fucking hypnotic. It was like just by looking at me she was clearing all the shit out of my brain. I wanted to cry. I felt it all rushing up through me like puke. I nodded, but I couldn't speak.

"Tell me," she said.

I still wanted to cry, but I swallowed it back down again. "I'm a junkie," I said. "I'm fucked up. I don't wanna be, but I can't help it. People offer me stuff and I can't say no. But I'm gonna get straight. I am. I'm gonna get straight and pull this band back together. I'll be a better bassist than that art school cunt, Matlock. We'll conquer the fucking world. We're the best fucking band there's ever been."

I stopped. It sounded like someone else talking. After a minute I said, "My head is fucked up. I don't know what's true and what isn't anymore. I don't know who I am."

"Who do you *think* you are?" she said. "Tell me everything. Let it all out."

"I'm Sid Vicious," I told her. "I'm a Sex Pistol. I'm a fucking star. I'm the bass player who can't play. I'm a joke. A pathetic junkie. I'm gonna live forever. I'm gonna be dead before I'm twenty-five. I fucking love Nancy. I can't live without her. She's fucked up my life. She's the worst thing that ever happened to me. John's my best mate. He looks out for me. I hate him and he hates me. He's got no future. I want him to fuck off. I love him. I don't wanna lose him. Everything's falling apart. Everything's turning to shit. We're gonna rule the fucking world. We're gonna be heroes. We're gonna destroy America. Malcolm's a fucking genius. Malcolm's a cunt who doesn't care about us. I'm gonna be a legend. I'm gonna be forgotten."

I couldn't stop. It was like cutting my arm and watching the blood spurt. I put a hand over my mouth to stop it pouring out of me. What I was saying was all true and all lies. It was everything and nothing, the good and the bad, the dream and the nightmare. They were different, but they were the same. It was all happening together, all at once, and I was stuck in the middle.

"You are at the crossroads, mon petit," the girl said.

"The crossroads, yeah," I said.

"Which way do you go from here?"

"I dunno."

She was staring at me, like she could see the thoughts fighting in my head. What was I? The bassist in the best fucking band in the world? Or a walking fuck-ing cliché, press fodder, Malcolm's fucking puppet? If I cleaned myself up, got myself together, we could be fucking huge, we could go down in fucking history as the band that changed music forever. But did I really want that? Did I wanna be a legend? Did I wanna be Elvis Presley twenty years from now, fat and ugly and useless, dying of a heart attack on a fucking toilet? Did I wanna be a dinosaur, like Led Zep and Pink Floyd and all that hippie shit? Did I wanna be a fucking *rock* star?

Fuck that. Fuck it all. I'd never be fucking *establishment*. But I'd find a way. My way.

The girl was still staring. Her eyes were glittering. At that moment she could've been an angel or a demon.

"It is your decision," she said.

"Is it?"

"Of course. If you want it to be."

"Can you help me?" I asked her.

Instead of answering, she stood up and held out her hand. "Come with me."

"Where we going?"

"To get you what you need."

I took her hand and she pulled me up like I weighed nothing.

"Noel and Glen are outside," I said. "They won't let me go."

She smiled. "Like I say, mon petit, I go where I please."

She pushed open the door and led me outside. Noel and Glen were sitting in the corridor playing cards. They didn't even look at us.

"Come," she said, and she gave me a little tug. I kept thinking that any second Noel would look up and say, "Where do you think you're going, Sid?"

But he didn't. Him and Glen just kept playing cards.

"What's wrong with 'em?" I whispered.

"They cannot see us," she said. "To them we are like the wind."

"Yeah?" I said. I walked right up and leaned over them. "Oi," I said.

They ignored me.

I laughed. It was like being a fucking superhero. The fucking invisible man. Noel had a can of beer on the floor by his chair. I picked it up and spat in it. He didn't respond.

"Oi, Noel," I said. "You're a fucking cunt."

He kept on playing cards.

I laughed again. And then suddenly I felt scared. I looked at the girl.

"Am I dead," I said. "Am I a ghost?"

She smiled. "No, mon petit."

"But no one can see me," I said. "I don't like it that no one can see me. I don't wanna be ignored."

The girl was still holding my hand. She leaned in and whispered in my ear, like it was a secret. "Trust me, mon petit."

I felt calm again. "Yeah," I said, "all right."

"Come," she said.

We went down the corridor and out through the stage door, into the main hall. There were still a lot of people around. Roadies, journalists, some fucking groupies and fans. I thought they'd turn round and look at us, but no one did. It was weird. It was good not being hassled, but I like it when people look at me. I like seeing their faces when they recognise me. Specially the birds.

There was no sign of Steve and Paul and Malcolm. I knew Steve and Paul were sick of all the driving, and earlier Steve had said he was gonna tell Malcolm that from now on he and Paul wanted to fly to the gigs like proper fucking pop stars, otherwise he'd fuck off home, so maybe that's what had happened.

John was still there, though. Still hunched over in the same place with his can of beer and his fag. He was surrounded by cunts hanging on his every fucking word, but as usual he looked bored and pissed off. He always took the piss out of me for being a "Daily Mirror punk," but he was just as bad. He was all right on the bus, then soon as he went out in public he turned into a moody, hostile cunt. Johnny Rotten, the punk rock star.

I was glad he was there, though. Glad he'd decided to stay with me and not fuck off with the others. Maybe it'd be easier with the others gone. Maybe we could be mates again. I hope so. Me and him, we're the real Sex Pistols. The others are just fucking wankers.

Me and the bird walked right across the room and no one even looked at us. We walked out of the room and out of the door and into the night.

It was fucking cold. Raining. Downtown Baton Rouge was a dump. The whole of America was a fucking dump. That bird had been right.

"Where we going?" I said. "I'm not fucking walking nowhere."

"Didn't I tell you to trust me?" the girl said, and she tugged on my hand again. "Come."

I don't like being told what to do, but with this girl it was all right. I didn't even wanna fuck her. Well, I did, but it would've been wrong. It would've been like fucking an angel or something.

She had a pick-up truck parked round the side of the club. An angel with a knackered fucking shitmobile of a pick-up truck. Ha fucking ha.

She opened the passenger door and told me to get in. I did. I was cold, shivering. She started the engine. It sounded like an old man coughing his guts up. I put the heater on, but I was still cold. But at least I didn't feel sick anymore. At least I didn't have stomach cramps. At least I wasn't itching.

"What's that smell?" I said.

"Crawfish. My brother is a fisherman. He supplies restaurants here in town and out in the bayou."

There was a fucked-up music system with a tape hanging out of it. I pushed the tape in and turned it on.

"What's this music?" I said.

"It's zydeco."

"Zydeco? What the fuck's that?"

"Roots music. You like it?"

"Yeah," I said. "It's good. It's like reggae, but faster."

"It's the music of the land," she said. "The music of the blood and the soul."

"Like the Sex Pistols," I said.

She smiled. "You think your Sex Pistols will play zydeco music?"

I grinned. "Yeah," I said. "Why fucking not?"

We drove out of town. It was just traffic lights and rain. The world looked like it was melting. The roads turned to dirt tracks. The truck bounced in and out of pot holes. Trees and swamps all round us. Shacks at the side of the road.

Then there weren't even any shacks. Just trees tangled together. Bent over and covered in slime. No stars, no moon, just darkness. I didn't know where we were and I didn't care.

The girl pulled over at the side of the track and turned off the engine. When the engine stopped the music did too. That's when I knew the sound of rusty violins weren't part of the music. They were insects screaming in the darkness.

She looked at me. Big brown eyes glowing.

"We're here," she said.

"Where?"

"At the crossroads."

"So where do we go now?"

"That's your decision, mon petit."

I got out of the truck. It had stopped raining. The trees dripped. The world still looked like it was melting. There was a smell of something old and rotting. I liked it here. It was dead, but it was away from the madness. Away from everything.

Something slithered in the darkness nearby and splashed into the water. I thought of the mayhem behind me. The blood and puke and shit and fights. The first sweet rush of smack through my veins and into my brain. I thought of all the people and the noise. The faces crowding me. Demon eyes and hungry mouths. Sucking my life away. Feeding on my corpse.

"I wanna stay here forever," I said.

"Which way, mon petit?" said the girl.

I turned round. Round and round on the spot. I didn't know what I was looking for, but then I saw it. A light through the trees. An orange glow. Like the moon had fallen out of the sky and was sinking into the swamp.

"There," I said. "Let's go there."

We walked towards the light. Insects made a noise like a thousand rusty doors creaking all at once. Things moved around us. I remembered Glen telling me on the bus about the animals they get here. Alligators and snakes and poisonous spiders. He told me hoping it would scare me. So I wouldn't run off to find some smack.

Well, fuck you. I'm Sid Vicious. I ain't gonna get eaten by no fucking alligator. I ain't scared of nothing. I'm the most dangerous fucking animal in America.

The light was farther away than it looked. We walked for ages, my boots splatting through mud and water. The girl walked next to me. She seemed to blend in, like she was part of the land. She moved silently, like she was floating.

The track got narrow. Water lapped on both sides of us. Things moved in the trees. Things splashed in the water. I thought of thousands of demon eyes watching us. Thousands of grinning mouths full of sharp teeth. I had no smack, no booze, nothing to keep the pain away. But I felt all right. The girl was my drug. My fucking angel.

Then the track widened into a clearing. In front of us was a wooden shack. It was raised up off the ground with a porch at the front. Orange light was shining out the front windows. Something flapped on the roof. Tarpaulin or plastic. When we got closer I saw the windows were covered in wire mesh. Big fucking moths were bouncing off them, desperate to get to the light.

I looked at the girl. The light was shining in her eyes, making them glow in the dark. She looked like a cat. A fucking leopard walking on two legs.

"Where are we?" I said. "Who lives here?"

"Why don't you find out, mon petit?"

I walked up the steps and knocked on the door. There was a sound from inside. A rusty old creak that might have been a voice. I pushed the door open. "Hello?"

The place was gloomy. Candles burning. Flickering shadows. Ratty old furniture. Wooden floor. It smelled old. Like old people. Dead and stale. There was no one here.

"Hello?" I shouted again. "Anyone home?"

There was a doorway at the back of the room. A big black opening. The shadows made it move and sway. It made me think of a mouth. An old man's mouth. No teeth. Yawning, struggling for breath. A voice came out of the mouth. Small and tired and creaky. It said something in a foreign language. French or something, I dunno.

I walked across to the door. Boots clomping on the wooden floor. I stuck my head through the opening, looked into the room. Couldn't see a fucking thing. Pitch black. I heard something moving, rustling.

"Who's there?" I said.

The scrape of a match. A flame. Behind the flame a yellow face, hanging in the darkness. The flame moved across, lit a candle. Light jumped into the room, surrounded by black moving shadows. The light was orangey-brown. There was a big bed and an old woman lying on it. She was fat and saggy. The light made her brown skin look shiny, like polished wood. She had bulging eyes. A big fuzz of black hair. The candle-light made the ends of her hair twitch like snakes.

"Hello," I said and grinned at her. "Who the fuck are you then?"

She said something else in a foreign language. I didn't know if it was her name or what.

"I ain't got a fucking clue what you're talking about," I said.

The girl spoke. I didn't even know she was behind me until I heard her voice. She said something foreign to the old woman and the old woman said something back. They spoke quickly. Jabba jabba jabba.

"What's she say?" I said.

"Her name is Madame Picou," said the girl. "She says she will help you."

"Madame what?" I said.

The girl spelled the old lady's name for me.

"Hello, Mrs. Picou," I said to the old lady. "I'm Sid."

The old lady said something. I shrugged.

"Madame Picou says take a seat," said the girl.

"All right, thanks," I said. There was a wooden chair under an old dressing table against the wall. I went over to it, and just for a second, when I looked in the mirror, I saw a skull looking back at me. I jumped and looked again. It was just me. In the candle-light my skin was white and my eyes were full of black shadows. I noticed things hanging off the sides of the mirror. Beads. Snake skins. I dragged the chair over to the bed and sat down.

The old lady jabbered again. She leaned towards me. She was so fat that she grunted like a pig as she rolled on to her side. A big fucking fart ripped out of her. I nearly pissed myself laughing. I was still laughing when she took my hands and looked at them, turning them over. Suddenly she shoved up the sleeves of my leather jacket and ran her fat thumbs up the insides of my arms.

I stopped laughing when I felt her stab something into my arm. Right into the fucking vein near my elbow. I was used to needles, but I wasn't expecting it and it made me jump.

"Ow!" I shouted and pulled my arm back. "What did you do that for, you cunt?"

I was angry. I wanted to smash something. Her face or her fucking furniture. I stood up and then I felt a hand on my shoulder, warm breath that smelt of spice and perfume against the side of my face.

"Hush, mon petit."

"She fucking stabbed me," I said.

"It is nothing," the girl said. "Relax."

My anger went away. Just like that. I sat down again. Suddenly I felt tired. Really tired. I couldn't move. I felt so relaxed that I couldn't even lift my hand from my leg.

"What's going on?" I said.

"It is nothing, mon petit," said the girl. "You are fine."

"I can't fucking move," I said.

"Madame Picou has paralysed you. But it is only temporary. Do not worry."

"What's she paralysed me for?"

"It is necessary."

"Why?"

Instead of answering me, the girl and the old bird jabbered at each other again. It seemed like the girl was asking questions and the old bird was giving her instructions, waving her arms about.

The girl went away. The old bird stared at me. Her face didn't move. She didn't blink.

"What you staring at?" I said.

She didn't answer.

Then the girl came back. She had some stuff in her hands. She put it on the bed.

There was a little doll made of string and cloth and twigs. A pair of scissors. A pin cushion. A little cloth bag. A bottle with some sort of liquid in it.

"What's going on?" I said.

The old bird put her finger to her lips and hissed at me.

"Shush yourself, you cunt," I said. "What's that? A fucking voodoo doll? You gonna put a curse on me or something?"

"It is a gris-gris," said the girl.

"What the fuck's that then?"

"It is to bind us together," she said.

"What do you mean?"

The girl took my hands and knelt in front of me. Usually when she touched me she made me feel calm. But I was getting scared and that made me angry. I'm a Sex Pistol. I ain't supposed to be scared of nothing.

"I need you, mon petit," the girl said. "I need you to save me."

"I thought *you* were gonna save *me*," I said.

"I would if I could, mon petit," said the girl. "But you are beyond redemption. I am sorry."

"Fuck off," I said. If I could've moved I would've smacked her one. But I couldn't, so I spat on her instead. My gob hit the side of her face. A big greeny. She just stayed where she was. Looked at me sadly and let it trickle down. Then she stood up.

She and the old bird jabbered some more. The old bird was waving her arms about, telling her what to do. The girl picked up the little doll. She got something out of her pocket and showed it to me. It was a picture of me, cut out of a newspaper. I was up on stage playing my bass. The girl pinned the picture of me to the little doll and gave it to the old woman. Then she picked up the scissors from the bed and came towards me.

"Fuck off," I said. "Get away from me." I spat at her again. It hit the front of her dress, but she ignored it.

I tried to move, but I was still fucking paralysed.

"You cut me and I'll fucking kill you," I said.

She reached out towards me. She made a sound through her teeth like she was trying to calm a fucking wild animal. When her hand got close enough I tried to bite it, but she was too quick. Her hand shot up and grabbed my hair.

"Fucking get off," I said.

She brought up the other hand with the scissors and cut a bit of my hair off.

"*Fuck off!*" I screamed at her. "*I'll fucking kill you, you bitch!*"

She held up the tuft of black hairs. Like she was showing me I didn't need to worry 'cos she'd only cut off a few. The old bird held up the doll, and the girl stuck the hairs to it. There was so much Vaseline on them that she didn't need glue or nothing. The old woman put the doll down on the bed and then picked up the little cloth bag and opened it. There was some sort of powder in it. I wasn't sure what it was, but it looked like smack. The old bird sprinkled some of the powder over the doll and started to jabber something in a foreign language. She closed her eyes and started to sway from side to side.

"What the fuck's she doing?" I said.

"Offering your image to the spirit," said the girl.

"What for?"

"So that we can seal the bond."

I shook my head. "What is this fucking bond? What are you doing to me? I ain't done nothing to you."

The girl looked at me. "I was like you, mon petit," she said.

"What do you mean?"

She pointed at the badge on my jacket. "I was a mess. I was ..." She mimed injecting a syringe into her arm.

"A junkie?"

She nodded. Behind her the old bird was still swaying and jabbering.

"And now you're clean?" I said.

The girl pulled a weird face. Like: not really. "You will *keep* me clean," she said.

"Oh yeah?" I said. "And how am I gonna do that?"

"By accepting my desire as your own."

I asked her what she meant, but she just smiled and turned round and went into the other room.

"Oi!" I shouted. "Don't fucking walk away from me! Come back here, you cunt!"

But she was gone. The old bird was still swaying and muttering. I could see her bulging eyes moving under her eyelids.

"And you can shut the fuck up as well," I said.

But she didn't. She just kept on and on. Jabba jabba jabba.

A few minutes later the girl came back. She'd taken all her clothes off. She was naked. Gorgeous. The most beautiful girl I had ever seen.

"Fuck," I said. "Are we gonna shag? Is that part of this voodoo shit?"

The girl smiled, but she didn't say anything. She came towards me. The light slid across her naked flesh. It was like she was made of golden oil. I didn't think it was possible for anyone to be so beautiful. I loved Nancy, but this girl made Nancy look like a skanky old slag. I didn't know whether I had a hard-on 'cos I couldn't feel anything from the neck down. But in my brain I had a hard-on. The biggest fucking hard-on in the world.

I sat there staring at her with my mouth open as the girl came over. My eyes couldn't get enough of her. I wanted to touch her so bad. Fuck all that angel stuff from before.

I was staring at her tits and cunt, so I didn't notice the tattoo at first. It was only when she started to pull my leather jacket off that I saw she had a tattoo of a thin black snake around her right arm.

"What's that?" I said.

"Le Grand Zombi," she replied.

"You what?"

"It is the serpent. It protects me from harm."

"Bollocks," I said. "Oi, what you doing with my jacket?"

She had my jacket off me now. She threw it on the bed at the old bird's fat ugly feet and looked at my arms.

"So many scratches, so many bruises," she said. She sounded sad. "Why do you hate yourself, mon petit?"

"I don't hate myself," I said. "I fucking love myself. I'm fucking brilliant, me."

I grinned at her, but she just looked sad. She turned away from me. Beautiful arse.

She picked up the little bottle and pulled the cork out of it. Then she started to shake out the liquid inside, spraying drops of it over the old bird and the voodoo doll.

The old bird didn't seem to mind. Didn't even notice.

The girl closed her eyes and started to jabber like the old woman. She started to dance too, her body rippling like a snake, her tits jiggling. She really got into it, went into a kind of trance. She shook more of the liquid over herself. Poured it over the snake tattoo on her arm, making it shine. Then she sprinkled the liquid over me, over *my* arm, the one I'd cut open. The wound had gone septic, but I couldn't feel it, not now. I looked at the arm as the liquid splashed over it, but only for a second. Looking at the girl's jiggling tits was much more fun.

Both of the fucking women were totally out of it now. Jiggling and jabbering.

All that ju-ju voodoo bollocks. The girl kept splashing liquid round. All over me, over her, over the old bird holding the doll.

"I'm fucking bored of this," I said loudly, but neither of them heard me.

The girl kept splashing water until the bottle was empty. Then she threw the bottle away.

The jabbering changed. It was creepy. It was like the two of them were linked together or something. Suddenly their voices got deeper. Slower. They started saying the same words. The old bird held out the doll and the girl grabbed it. They both clung to it like a couple of kids fighting over a toy. The girl reached out with her other arm and grabbed my hand. I couldn't do nothing about it. We were like a human chain. The old bird and the girl still swaying and jiggling like nutters.

"What is this? Ring a ring of fucking roses?" I said.

Then the snake tattoo on the girl's arm started to move. I thought it was just the light at first, or my eyes, or that fucking stuff the old bird had injected into me fucking up my head.

"Fucking hell," I said. I squeezed my eyes shut, then opened them again. The snake tattoo was still moving. The thin black snake was curling down the girl's arm like a stripe on a fucking barber's pole. Down towards her wrist. Towards her hand. Towards *my* hand.

I tried to break free, but I couldn't move. I shouted and spat at her, but it made no difference.

The snake tattoo wasn't a tattoo no more. It was a real snake. It made a rustling sound when it moved. Its tongue flickered in and out. Its little yellow eyes fucking stared at me.

I yelled out when it moved from the girl's hand on to my hand. Then it was coiling up my arm. Taking its time. I couldn't feel it, but I could see it. I moved my head back as far as I could, terrified it was going to come all the way up my arm and bite me in the neck like a fucking vampire. Maybe it'd eat my eyes. Or crawl down my fucking throat and choke me. Maybe it'd go inside me and lay eggs and loads of baby snakes would hatch out and eat their way out of my stomach. I screamed at them to get the fucking thing off me, but they were still out of it, jiggling and chanting.

The snake moved up my arm to just above my elbow. Then it stopped. It gathered in its coils, bunched up. Now it looked like the belt I wrapped round my arm when I wanted to find a vein. The snake tightened round my arm until a big blue vein popped up in my elbow. I could see the vein pulsing away. Slowly the snake lifted its head. Then it struck. It opened its mouth wide and sank its fucking fangs right into the vein.

I screamed. I couldn't feel nothing, but I screamed.

"*Get it off, you bitches! Get this fucking thing off me!*"

My voice sounded weird in my own head. Rough and echoing. Like it was someone else's voice shouting from down the end of a long metal tunnel. My body was still paralysed, but my arm felt hot. I thought of the snake's venom mixing with my blood. Rushing through my body, travelling to my heart and my brain. I wondered if I was gonna die. The thought of dying didn't seem too bad. If I died on tour I'd get in the papers. I'd be on the front page. Yeah, that'd be all right.

My thoughts were falling apart. The room pulsed in and out, getting small then big, bright then dim. I didn't know the two birds had stopped their voodoo bollocks until the girl knelt in front of me. She took my hands. She smiled at me. Face shiny with sweat. Big brown eyes glowing. Even now she was beautiful. She'd fucking killed me, but she was beautiful.

"The snake is my desire, mon petit," she said. "You must feed my desire as well as your own. This way only one of us will die."

I could hardly keep my eyes open. My head was like a heavy rock. I tried to speak. I heard the words in my head, but I don't know if she did.

"Fuck you," I said.

Then it all went black. When I woke up it was dark and I was shivering. There was a hammering sound. Voices.

"Sid! Sid!"

I didn't realise I could move until I sat up. I felt like shit. Body aching, full of cramps. Covered in cold sweat. Arm, chest, and bollocks itching like crazy.

I looked around. My head felt full of broken glass. I was in the broom cupboard in the Kingfish Club. The cupboard where I'd shagged the bird. The cupboard where the girl had come to me.

There was no one here now. Just me.

"Sid! Sid!"

"What?" I shouted.

The door opened. It was Noel.

"We're all packed up, Sid. Ready to move on."

"Where we fucking going?" I said.

"Dallas, Sid. We're going to Dallas. Come on, man. You want a hand?"

Noel came into the room and helped me up. I rushed over to the sink and puked my guts out.

"You okay, Sid," Noel said.

"No, I feel fucking terrible," I said. "I need some stuff, Noel. I need it now."

"No stuff, Sid. You know that. Soon as we get on the bus you can have some valium. How's that sound?"

I wasn't listening. I remembered what the girl had said. "You must feed my desire as well as your own."

I took my leather jacket off. Curled around my arm was the little black snake. It lifted its head and flicked its tongue at me. I screamed.

"Jesus, Sid," Noel said. "What's wrong?"

"*Get it off me, Noel!*" I yelled. "*Fucking get it off me!*"

"Get what off you, Sid?" Noel asked.

I held my arm out. "*The snake! Get the fucking snake off!*"

Noel looked at my arm. "There's no snake, Sid," he said. "You're hallucinating, man. Come on."

He walked out of the room. I looked at the snake wrapped around my arm. The snake only I could see. I looked at the blue vein pulsing in the crook of my elbow, and in that second I knew.

I was lost. Lost for good. There was no way back.

Feed the snake, I thought. *Feed the fucking snake.*

I put my leather jacket on and followed Noel out of the room.

Death Stopped for Miss Dickinson

By

Kristine Kathryn Rusch

January 26, 1863
Near Township Landing, Florida

The air smelled of pine trees, a scent Colonel Thomas Wentworth Higginson associated with home. Here, in the Florida, where dark, spindly trees rose around him like ghosts, Higginson never imagined he'd be thinking of Massachusetts, with its stately settled forests and its magnificent tamed land.

Nothing was tamed here. His boots had been damp for days, the earth mushy, even though his regiment, the First South Carolina Volunteer Infantry, had somehow found solid ground. He could hear the tramp, tramp, tramp of hundreds of feet, but his soldiers were quiet, well trained, alert.

Everything Washington, D.C., thought they would not be.

Even in the dark, after days of river travel, Higginson was proud of these men, the most disciplined he had ever worked with. He said so in his dispatches, although he doubted Union Command believed him. They had taken a risk creating an entire regiment of colored troops, mostly freed slaves, all of whom had been in a martial mood much of the month, ever since word of President Lincoln's Emancipation Proclamation reached them.

A strange clip-clop, then the whinny of a horse, and a shushing. Higginson's breath caught. His men had no horses. They traveled mostly on steamers, and hence had no need of horses, even if the Union Army had deemed such soldiers worthy of steeds—which they did not.

He whispered a command. It was all he needed to stop his troops. They halted immediately and slapped their rifles into position.

He had a fleeting thought that made him smile—a Confederate soldier's worst nightmare: to meet a black man with a gun—and then waited.

The silence was thick, the kind of silence that came only when men listened, trying to hear someone else move. Breathing hushed, each movement monitored. No one wanted to move first.

Then Higginson saw him, rising out of the trees as if made of smoke—a black-robed figure, face hidden by a hood, carrying a scythe.

Higginson's breath caught. What kind of madness was this? Some kind of farmer lurking in the woods, killing soldiers?

The figure turned toward him. In the darkness, the hood looked empty. Higginson saw no face, just a great, gaping beyond.

His heart pounded. He was forty years old, tired, overworked and over-wrought; hallucinations should not have surprised him.

But they did, *this* did.

And then the hallucination dissolved as if it had never been. One of his men cried out, and a volley of shots lit up the night, revealing nothing where the hooded figure had stood.

All around it, however, horses, men, Confederates—white faces in the strange gunlight, looking frightened and surprised. They surrounded his men, but could not believe what they saw—for a moment anyway.

Then their weapons came out, and they returned fire, and Higginson forgot the hooded figure, forgot that moment of silence, and plunged deep into the battle, his own rifle raised, bayonet out as, around him, the air filled with the stink of gunpowder, the screams of horses, the wild cries of men.

The battle raged late into the night and when it was done, rifle smoke hung in the sky, the trees nearly invisible, the wounded crying around him. Thirteen bodies—twelve of theirs, one of his—gathered nearer each other than he would have liked.

Near the spot where he had seen the hooded figure, where he had imagined smoke, in that moment of silence, before the first shot was fired and the first smoke appeared.

Forty years old and he had never been frightened—not when he attacked Boston's courthouse trying to rescue escaped slave Anthony Burns, not when he fought with the free-staters in Kansas, not when he met John Brown with an offer to fund the raid on Harper's Ferry.

No, Thomas Wentworth Higginson had never been frightened, not until he saw those bodies, scattered in a discernable pattern in the ghostly wood where a spectral figure had stood hours before, and wielded a scythe, creating a clearing where Higginson would have sworn there had not been one before.

He reassured himself: every man was allowed one moment of terror in a war. Then he resolved that he would never be frightened again.

And he was not. In the war, anyway.

But he would be frightened again, and much worse than this, in a small town in Massachusetts where he met a slight poetess, seven years later.

May 23, 1886
The Homestead
Amherst, Massachusetts

Lavinia Dickinson stood in the doorway to her sister's bedroom. It still smelled faintly of Emily—liniment and homemade lavender soap, dried leaves from the many plants she'd preserved, and of course, the sharp odor of India ink that seemed embedded in the walls.

The bed was bare, the coverings washed and to be washed again. Dr. Bigelow had initially said Emily died of apoplexy, but he had written on her death certificate that she had been a victim of Bright's Disease, which he swore had no contagion.

Vinnie had learned, in her fifty-three years, that doctors knew less than most about death and disease, but she trusted Dr. Bigelow enough to keep the sheets and Emily's favorite quilt, although she would launder them repeatedly before putting them away.

Vinnie had thought to burn them, but their mother had made that quilt, and it held precious memories. Still, Vinnie had time to change her mind. She would have a bonfire soon, before the summer dryness set in.

Emily had made her swear—had asked a solemn oath—that Vinnie would destroy her papers, *all* her papers, should Emily die first.

Vinnie had not expected Emily to die first. That bright flame seemed impossible to distinguish, even as she lay unconscious on her bed for two days, her breath coming in deep unnatural rasps.

No one expected Emily to die—least of all, Emily.

And Vinnie was uncertain how to proceed, without her stronger, smarter, older sister to guide her.

May 15, 1847
The West Street House
Amherst, Massachusetts

The moon cast an eerie silver light through Emily's bedroom window. She set down her pen and blew out the candle on her desk. The light seemed stronger than before.

She slid her chair back, the legs scraping against the polished wood floor, and paused for a moment, hoping she had not awakened Father. He would tell her she should sleep more, but of late, sleep eluded her. She felt on the cusp of something—what, she could not tell. Something life-changing, though.

Something soul-altering.

She dared not speak these thoughts aloud. When she had uttered less controversial thoughts, her mother chided her and urged her to pull out her Bible when blasphemy threatened to overtake her. Emily's father did not censure her thoughts, but he looked concerned, worrying that the books he bought her had weakened her girlish mind.

All except her father and her brother Austin recommended church, hoping the Lord would speak to her and she would become saved. She saw no difference between those who had become saved and those who had not, except, perhaps, a certain smugness. She was smug enough, she liked to tell her sister Lavinia. Vinnie would smile reluctantly, at both the truth of the statement and the sheer daring of it.

Everyone they knew waited to be saved; that her brother and father had not yet achieved this was seen as a failing in their family, not as something to be emulated. If she was not saved, she would not reunite with her family in Heaven. Indeed, she might not go to Heaven.

And, at times, such an idea did not terrify her. In fact, it often filled her with relief.

Eternity, she had once said to Vinnie, *appears dreadful to me.*

Vinnie did not understand, nor did Austin. And Emily couldn't quite convey how often she wished Eternity did not exist. The idea of living forever, in any way—*to never cease to be*, as she had said to Vinnie—disturbed her in her most quiet moments.

Like now. That silver light made her think of Eternity, perhaps because the silver made the light seem unnatural somehow.

She crept to the window, crouching before it, her hand on the sill, and peered out.

Behind their home lay Amherst's burial ground. The poor and the unshriven slept here, alongside the colored and those not raised within the confines of a Christian household. Oftimes she sat in her window and watched as families mourned or as a sexton dug a grave for a lonesome and already forgotten soul.

On this night, the graves were bathed in unnatural light. The world below looked silver, except for the darkness lurking at the edges. Something had leached all of the color from the ground, the stones, and the trees behind—yet the bleakness had a breathtaking beauty.

In the midst of it all, a young man walked, hands clasped behind him as if he were deep in thought. Although he assumed the posture of a scholar, his muscular arms and shoulders spoke of a more physical toil—farmer, perhaps, or laborer. Oddly the light did not make his shirt flare white. Instead, its well-tailored form looked as black as the darkness at the edges of the cemetery. His trousers too, although she was accustomed to black trousers. All the men in her life wore them.

He paced among the graves as if measuring the distance between them, pausing at some, and staring at the others as if he knew the soul inside.

Emily leaned forward, captivated. She had seen this man before, but in the churchyard in the midst of a funeral. He had leaned against an ornate headstone, resting on one of the cherubim encircling the stone's center.

She had expected someone to chase him off—after all, one did not lean against gravestones, particularly as the entire congregation beseeched the Lord to send a soul to its rest.

But he had for just a brief moment. Then, perhaps realizing he had been seen, he moved—vanished, she thought that day, because she did not see him among the mourners.

Although she saw him now.

As if he overheard the thought, he raised his head. He had a magnificently fine face, strong cheekbones, narrow lips, dramatic brows curving over dark eyes. Those eyes met hers, and her breath caught. She had been found out.

He smiled and extended a hand.

For a moment, she wanted nothing more than to clasp it.

But she sat until the feeling passed.

She ran to no one. She did no one's bidding, not even her father's. While she tried to be a dutiful daughter, she was not one.

And she would not run to a stranger in the burial ground, no matter how beautiful the evening.

No matter how lovely the man.

May 23, 1886
The Homestead
Amherst, Massachusetts

Piles of papers everywhere. Vinnie sat cross-legged on the rag rug no one had pulled out during spring cleaning—Emily had been too sick to have her room properly aired—and stared at the sewn booklets she had found hidden in Emily's bureau.

Once their mother had thought the bureau would house Emily's trousseau, back when the Dickinsons believed even their strange oldest daughter would marry well and bring forth children, as God commanded. But she had not, and neither had Vinnie. Austin had married well, or so it seemed at first, although he and Sue were now estranged, a condition made worse by the untimely death of their youngest child, Gib.

Vinnie wished Emily had given Austin this task. Emily lived in her words. She had better friends on paper than she had in person. She wrote letters by the bucketful, and scribbled alone late into the night. To destroy Emily's correspondence, Vinnie thought, would be like losing her sister all over again.

And yet Vinnie had been prepared to do it, until she discovered the booklets. Hand-sewn bundles of papers, with individual covers. Inside, the papers were familiar: Emily's poems. But oh, so many more than Vinnie had ever imagined.

Emily gifted family and friends with her poems, sometimes in letters, sometimes folded into a whimsical package. Her tiny careful lettering at times made the poem difficult to discern, but there, upon the page, were little moments of Emily's thoughts. Anyone who knew her could hear her voice resound off the pages:

I'm nobody, she said in her wispy childlike voice. *Who are you? Are you nobody, too?*

Vinnie could almost see her, crouching beside her window, watching the children play below. More than once, she had sent them a basket of toys from above, but had not played with them.

Instead, she preferred to watch or participate at a great distance.

But once she had been a child, with Vinnie.

Then there's a pair of us, Emily said. *Don't tell! They'd banish us, you know.*

The poems had no date, and Emily's handwriting looked the same as always. Her cautious, formal handwriting, not the scrawl of her early drafts.

These poems had meant something to her. She had sought to preserve them.

Vinnie closed the booklet, and clutched it to her bosom.

Emily lived inside these books. However, then, could Vinnie destroy them?

May 19, 1847
The West Street House
Amherst, Massachusetts

The silver light returned four nights later. It was not tied to the moon as Emily had thought because, as she headed up the stairs to her room, she noted clouds forming on the horizon.

The night had been dark until the light appeared.

Instead of peering out her window, she slipped on her shoes and hurried down the stairs. Her father read in the library. Her mother cleaned up the kitchen from the evening meal. Her older brother Austin, home from school, sat at the desk in the front parlor, composing a letter. He did not look up as she passed.

She let herself out the front, simply so that her mother would not see her.

Cicadas sang. The air smelled of spring—green leaves and fresh grass and damp ground. All familiar scents, familiar sounds. The music of her life.

The strange silver light did not touch the front of the house. Perhaps the light came from some kind of powerful lantern, one she had not seen that night.

She stole around the house, her heart pounding. She never went out at night, except when accompanied, and only when it was required. A concert, a meeting, a request to witness one of her father's legal documents.

Unmarried girls did not roam the grounds of their home, even if they were sixteen and worldly wise. She was not worldly wise, although she was cautious.

And now what she was doing felt forbidden, deliciously daring, and exciting.

She rounded the corner into the back yard. The silver light flowed over the burial ground, but did not touch the Dickinson property. The darkness began at the property line, which she found passing strange.

But as she stepped onto the grass behind her house, the silver light caught her white dress, making it flare like a beacon.

She froze, heart pounding. Revealed. Her hands shook, and she willed them to stop.

She had nothing to be afraid of, she told herself. The burial ground was empty except for the light.

She tiptoed forward, trying not to rustle the grass. She kept her breathing even and soft. She had seen deer move this way, silently through thick foliage. The grass was not thick here. The yardman kept it trim for the Dickinsons, the sexton for the burial ground.

Yet she felt as if she were being watched. The hair rose on the back of her neck, and in spite of her best efforts, her heart rate increased.

It took all of her concentration to keep her breathing steady.

To walk in a graveyard at night. What kind of ghost or demon was she trying to summon?

All of Amherst already thought her strange. Would they think her even stranger if they saw her wandering through the graves, her white dress making her seem ghostly and ethereal?

Something moved beside her. She looked over her shoulder, half expecting Austin, arms crossed, a frown on his face. *What are you doing?* he'd ask in a voice that mimicked Father's.

Only Austin wasn't there.

No one was there.

She wanted to run back to the house, but she made herself walk forward, to that small patch of ground where she had seen the man four nights before. The graves there were not fresh. One had sunken slightly. Another had flattened against the earth. A third had a stone so old that the carvings had become unreadable. The light seemed stranger here than it had from the window, leaching the color from her skin. She seemed fanciful, a phantom herself. If someone saw her, they might not think they were seeing young Miss Dickinson, but a specter instead.

Something rose behind one of the ancient tilting headstones—a column of smoke, no!—a man dressed all in black, a cowl over his head, a scythe in his hand.

Emily fled across the grass, careful to avoid sinking graves, her breath coming in great gasps. She was halfway to the house before she caught herself.

It was, she thought, a trick of the light, and nothing more. She had expected to see a phantom in the graveyard and so she had—the worst of all phantoms, that old imperator, Death.

She made herself turn. She was not frightened of anything, and she would not flee like a common schoolgirl from phantoms in the darkness.

Behind her, the sky was clear, the silver light still filling the burial ground. But there was no column of smoke, no cowled figure, no scythe.

There was, however, that handsome young man, leaning on a gravestone that looked like it might topple at any moment.

He smiled at her again, and her traitorous heart leapt in anticipation. But she knew better than to approach him—not because she was afraid of him; she wasn't—but because she knew once she spoke, this illusion of interest and attraction would fade, and he would see her as all the others had, as intense and odd and unlikable.

"Emily Elizabeth Dickinson," he said, his voice a rich baritone. "Look at you. 'She walks in beauty, like the night.'"

His use of her name startled her. That he so easily quoted Lord Byron startled her all the more. A literate man, and one not afraid of showing his knowledge of the more scandalous poets.

She straightened her shoulders so that she stood at her full height, which wasn't much at all. She knew some often mistook her for a child; she was so slight and small.

"You have me at a disadvantage, sir," she said. "You know of me, but I do not know of you."

His smile was small. "I know of many people who do not know me," he said. "In fact, I am astounded that you can see me at all."

"'Tis the strange light, sir," she said. "It illuminates everything."

"That it does," he said. "You should not be able to see it, either."

He was strange, from his word choice to his conversation to his decision to lean against a gravestone. Was this how others saw her? Strange, unpredictable, something they had never encountered before?

"If by that you mean I should not be out here among the graves, you are probably right," she said. "But it is a beautiful evening, and I fancied a walk."

He laughed. "You fancied me."

She raised her chin ever so slightly. "I beg your pardon, sir."

"I did not mean that like it sounds," he said. "You saw me four nights ago, and you came to see what I was doing."

He had caught her again. "Perhaps I did, sir," she said. "What of it?"

"Aren't you going to ask me what I'm doing here?" he asked.

"Mourning, I would assume," she said. "I did not mean to intrude upon your grief."

"You're not," he said. "I am not grieving. I am just visiting my dead."

Blunt words, harsh words, but true words. He was a kindred soul. Her entire family constantly admonished her for her harsh speech. But, she said, she preferred truth to socially acceptable lies.

It seemed, however, that others did not.

She took a step toward him. His eyes twinkled, which surprised her. Before she had thought them dark and deep, unfathomable. The hint of light in them was unexpected.

"Why visit at night?" she asked. "Wouldn't it be better to come here during the day?"

"Yes, it would," he said. "But daylight is not available to me. So I bring my own."

His hand moved, as if he were indicating the silver light. But it seemed to have no obvious source. If he had command of the silver light, then he also had command of the moonlight, something no mortal could possibly have.

So she dismissed his talk as fanciful. But intriguing. Everything about him was intriguing.

He tilted his head as he looked at her. There was a power in his gaze she had never encountered before. It drew her, like it had drawn her that first night. But she was suspicious of power and charisma, much as it attracted her.

"The real question," he said, "is not why I'm here, but why you're here."

"We've already discussed that, sir. I came to investigate the light."

"Ah, yes," he said softly. "But how did you see this light?"

"Sir?" The question disturbed her, and she wasn't quite sure why. She certainly wasn't going to tell him that her bedroom overlooked the burial ground. The fact that he had seen her in her room was already an invasion of privacy no one she knew would approve of.

"This," he said, sweeping his hand again—indicating the graves instead of the light? Had she mistook the gesture?—"should all be invisible to you for another forty years."

She laughed at his naiveté. Death surrounded them always, didn't he know that?

"Death, sir," she said primly, and saw him start at the word, "is all we know of heaven. And all we need of hell."

His smile faded, and so did the light in his eye. "True enough," he said. "So. Don't I frighten you?"

He attracted her; he did not frighten her.

"I suppose you should," she said. "But you do not."

"Amazing," he said softly. "You are truly amazing."

He stood, dusted off the back of his trousers, and nodded at her, his mouth in a determined line.

"This meeting is inappropriate," he said.

She shrugged, no longer uncomfortable. "I have found that most of what I do is inappropriate," she said, wondering if she should admit such a thing to a man she had just met. "I did not mean to compromise you."

He laughed. The sound boomed across the stones. "Compromise me." He bowed slightly, honoring her. "You are a treasure, Miss Dickinson."

"And you are a mystery, sir," she said.

He nodded. "The original mystery in fact," he said. "And I think that for tonight, we shall leave it that way. Good night, Miss Dickinson."

Dismissed, then. Well, she was used to that. People could not stomach her presence long.

"Good night, sir," she said, and slowly, reluctantly, made her way back to the house.

August 16, 1870
The Homestead
Amherst, Massachusetts

Thomas Wentworth Higginson called her his partially cracked poetess. He knew, long before he traveled to the Dickinson home in Amherst, that the woman who wrote to him was different. He had many words for her—wayward, difficult, fascinating.

But none of them prepared him for what he found.

He arrived on a hot August afternoon, expecting conversation about literature and publication and poetry. He preferred literary conversation; he tried not to think about the war, although it haunted him. He dreamed of boots tramping on damp ground, of neighing horses, and startled men.

But he woke, panicked, whenever he saw the hooded figure approach, shrouded in darkness, carrying a scythe.

The Dickinson house itself was beautiful, easily the finest house in Amherst. Two vast stories, built in the Federal style, with an added cupola and a conservatory. Higginson had not expected such finery, including the extensive white fence, the broad expanse of grounds, and the steps leading up to the gate.

He felt, for the first time in years, as if he had not dressed finely enough, as if his usual suit coat and trousers, light worsted to accommodate the summer heat, was too casual for a family that could afford a house like this.

But he had known some of the greatest people in the country, and he had learned that finery did not always equal snobbery. So he rapped on the door with confidence, removing his hat as the door swung open.

A woman no longer young opened the door. Her eyes were bright, her chestnut hair pulled away from her round cheeks. She smiled welcomingly, and said, "You must be Colonel Higginson."

"At your service, ma'am," he said, bowing slightly.

She giggled, which surprised him, and said, "We do not stand on ceremony here, sir. I am Lavinia Dickinson. I'll fetch my sister for you."

She beckoned him to step inside, and so he did with a bit of relief that this clear-eyed, normal girl was not his poetess. He would have been disappointed if she had been wrapped in a predictable façade.

The entry was a wood-paneled room, dark and oppressive after the bright summer light. Lavinia Dickinson delivered him to the formal parlor dotted with lamps, marking it as a house filled with readers. He sat on the edge of the settee as Lavinia Dickinson disappeared behind a door, leaving him, hat in hand, to await instruction. He felt like a suitor rather than an accomplished man who had come to visit one of his correspondents.

Eight years of letters with Emily, as she bid him to call her. Eight years of poems and criticisms and comments. Eight years, spanning his war service and his homecoming, two moves, and changes he had never been able to imagine.

Still, her letters arrived with their tiny handwriting and their startling poems. He had looked forward to this meeting for months now, had tried to stage it for a few years. But the poetess herself rarely left Amherst and he rarely traveled there.

His hands ached slightly, and he unclenched his fingers so that he did not crush his hat.

The house unsettled him; at least, that was what he thought at first. But as the moments wore on, he realized his unease came from the whispers around him, and then something stirring in the air, like a strong rain-scented wind arriving before a storm.

The door banged open, and the storm arrived. She was tiny, with her red hair pulled into two smooth bands. Her plain white dress made her seem young—it was a girl's dress—but the blue net worsted shawl over it was an older woman's affectation. She clutched two day lilies in one fist.

He would have thought her childlike if not for her eyes. They glowed. His breath caught, and he stood a half second too late. He had seen eyes like that before, although not nearly as manic, when he sat across from the militant abolitionist John Brown, whose raid on Harper's Ferry had helped start the war.

Higginson, along with five friends, had funded that raid. He would not have done so if he hadn't believed in Brown and his extreme methods. Most people had been frightened of the man, but Higginson hadn't been. He had thought then that Brown, whom some later called crazy, had the light of God in his eyes.

Higginson did not think God existed in Emily Dickinson's eyes. An odd silver light looked through him, and even though she smiled, she did not seem warm.

She thrust the flowers at him and said, "Forgive me if I'm frightened—"

She didn't seem frightened to him. She seemed excited, like a child about to receive a treat for good behavior. She held part of herself in check, but the excitement overpowered her control, making her jitter.

"—but I hardly see strangers and I don't know what to say."

That didn't stop her. She started talking, but he had trouble listening; all he could do was focus on those eyes. Killer eyes. He had seen eyes like that in some Rebel soldiers as they bayoneted his men. He made himself breathe, made himself listen, made himself converse, but he scarcely remembered what he said.

She introduced him to her father—a colorless old man, without much humor—and invited her sister to join them, but her sister demurred.

Instead, Higginson was stuck with Emily. He felt something drain from him as she talked, a bit of his life essence, as if being around her took something from him. It took all of his considerable strength just to hold his own against her.

The comparison to a storm wasn't even apt. She wasn't a summer storm, filled with rain and thunder. She was a tornado, sweeping in and seizing all around her. Only his encounter with her did not last an instant; it lasted hours.

And when it was finally finished, he staggered out of that strange house, relieved to be gone, and thrilled that she had not touched him. It took all of his strength to hold the day lilies she had given him. The day lilies and the photograph of Elizabeth Barrett Browning's grave.

Emily had smiled at him, a strange, sad, pathetic little smile, and said she was grateful because he had saved her life.

He hadn't saved her life. He hadn't done anything except read her poetry. He had even told her not to publish it because he thought it undisciplined, like her. Or so he had initially thought.

But that evening, as he sat alone in his rented room, trying to find words to express to his wife the strangeness of the experience, he realized that Miss Emily Dickinson hadn't been undisciplined. She hadn't been undisciplined at all.

In fact, it seemed to him, she was one of the most disciplined people he had ever met, as though explosions constantly erupted inside her and she had to keep them contained.

I never was with any one who drained my nerve power so much, he finally wrote to his wife. *Without touching her, she drew from me. I am glad not to live near her.*

He couldn't write any more. He didn't dare tell Mary that he felt Emily Dickinson had taken something vital from him, that talking to her had made him feel as if he were one step closer to death.

December 18, 1854
The West Street House
Amherst, Massachusetts

Emily woke up in his arms, cradled against his chest. This man, who seemed so otherworldly, was warm and passionate. His breathing was even, regular, but try as she might, she could not hear his heart beat.

She tried not to think of that, just like she tried not to think about what she was letting him do, sneaking into her room, lying naked in her bed. Her father had never caught him here, and she used to be afraid of what her father would do.

But now she didn't have that fear. Now she was afraid of what this man would do, this man who carried silver light with him as if he held a lantern.

The light did come when he summoned it, just like he had said to her. And it fled when he asked it to leave. The darkness around him without the light was absolute. She felt safe with him, in that darkness, but when he left, terror came.

And he always left before dawn.

He could not handle the light—real light. Daylight.

Her time with him would lessen as summer came, just like it always had. They lived best in winter, together.

She knew what he was. She watched him, after he left her, fading as his light faded, disappearing into the absolute darkness he created. Over time, some of his silver light spilled into her and she could see in the dark better than a cat could.

She could see him don his cowl, and pick up his scythe.

The nights he left early, the nights he arrived late, changed Amherst as well. The days after those nights she heard stories of breathing ceased, and hearts stopped, and sometimes she saw the funerals in the graveyard beneath her window, and she knew they happened because he had been there. He had touched someone.

Not like he touched her.

She was different, or so he said, had been different from the day they met. She should not have been able to see him, not until she was nearly dead herself.

But she was beginning to think she was not alive, not really, that something inside her had died long before she had found him, that her spirit had vanished, that she had no soul.

Surely, she did not feel the stirrings her family felt at revivals, and she did not feel the call of God. She understood He existed, but at a distance, not as someone who could live within her heart.

In earlier times, less enlightened times, here in Massachusetts, they would have called her a witch.

She knew this, and this man, this man who held her, he confirmed it, declaring himself lucky to have found her.

"Love," he said, "does not come to us often."

And by "us," he did not mean her and him. He meant himself and others like him, those whom everyone else called Death. She was not sure whom he worked for—the Devil? Or some unnatural demon? Or Heaven itself? For as she had said to him in their first conversation, Heaven would not exist without him.

Death had to occur before it could be overcome. And she could not die.

Or so she believed.

She pressed herself against his warm skin, losing herself in his familiarity.

To remain alive forever—to live for Eternity—to be Immortal: those things terrified her. She did not discuss them with him, because he thought them good, and she did not want to hurt him.

But he wanted her at his side forever.

And forever, to her, was much too long.

There are, he said to her once—just once—*a thousand ways to live forever. The soul must be preserved.*

Caught like a butterfly in a jar? she asked.

He shook his head, and smiled his beautiful smile at her fancy. *Recorded,* he said. *The soul must find permanence somewhere. Memory fades and eventually souls do as well. Except for a select few, kept alive in word or deed or a powerful magic.*

Have you that magic? she asked.

Sometimes, he said. *I could preserve you.*

No, she said too quickly. Then calmer, as if it didn't frighten her, *No. I prefer to sleep. I don't want Eternity.*

You are the only one then, he said.

Do you have it? she asked.

Yes, he said. *And I would like to share it with you.*

She shuddered. *Promise me you won't. When the time comes. Promise me.*

But he wouldn't promise. And that silence lay like ashes inside her heart.

May 24, 1886
The Homestead
Amherst, Massachusetts

The room had become a pile of papers. Vinnie covered every bare surface with poetry, all written by her sister. Vinnie had finally counted the sheets—counted and recounted and counted again.

Each time, she got a different number, but each time, the number staggered her. At least a thousand.

At least.

And such poems! About things Emily should not have known. Secret things. Intimate things.

Things that made Vinnie blush as she read them, hearing—despite her best intentions—Emily's voice:

You left me, sweet—Emily never called anyone sweet, and yet here it was, an endearment, casual as if she spoke it often—*two legacies. A legacy of love a Heavenly Father would content had He had the offer of....*

Emily, writing of love, the kind of love that men and women had, not love that friends or family had. Vinnie knew that, not because of the word *love*, but because of the other legacy, the one she could hear clearest in Emily's voice, the one that made her sound bitter and frightened and just a little lost:

You left me boundaries of pain, Emily said, *capacious as the sea. Between eternity and time, your consciousness and me.*

Emily was so afraid of eternity, so averse to time that she did not learn how to read a clock until she was fifteen. Time scarcely touched her, not even near the end. She always looked like a girl. Others aged, but Emily remained as youthful as she had been when they moved from the West Street House to the Homestead. She had been perhaps twenty-five or so, a young woman surely, but one trapped in amber.

Vinnie aged, going from a plump young woman to a matronly old maid. Austin had become serious, his face falling into lines that aged him prematurely.

But Emily, in her white dresses, remained the same—at least on the outside.

And who knew what had gone on inside? Clearly Vinnie hadn't. And Vinnie thought she had known her sister as a maid, not as someone who could write, *Wild nights! Wild nights! Were I with thee, wild nights should be our luxury!*

What had Vinnie missed all those years? Were the townspeople of Amherst right and Vinnie wrong? Had Emily locked herself in the house because she pined for a man who left her? Had she truly been one of those women who, like Miss Havisham of *Great Expectations*, had lost herself because of a man?

How could Vinnie have not known that? How could Vinnie have not known about the man?

She sat among her sister's papers, and tried to remember. But the poems were undated and gave her no clue—except that her sister, whom Vinnie thought she knew well, had become a mystery, one Vinnie was beginning to think she would never understand.

October 30, 1855
The West Street House
Amherst, Massachusetts

He sat on the edge of her bed, splendid in his nakedness. Was he splendid because he was immortal? Or had he been splendid in life?

Emily was afraid to ask him. She had learned that direct questions made him glare at her with those empty death-filled eyes.

Some questions she left unasked. Others she danced around, got answers to. Sometimes he just told her unbidden, told her of his extreme loneliness, and how pleased he was to have found a kindred soul.

That was what he called her. A kindred soul.

And of late, Vinnie told her that in certain light, her eyes turned silver.

Emily shuddered and pulled the blanket around her before leaning against his naked back. He bent at the waist, his hands in his thick black hair.

"You have to stop it," he said in desperation. She had never heard this tone in his voice before.

"I can't," she said. "We're moving. Father has decreed it."

He shook his head. "You have to change your father's mind."

"It's not possible," Emily said. "My grandfather built that house. He lost it. My father has waited his entire life to buy it back."

His tone frightened her; his whole demeanor frightened her. She had never been frightened of him before.

But she continued to lean against him, trying to draw strength from his warm skin.

"I can't visit you there," he said, his voice shaking. "Not until...."

"Until?" she asked.

"Not for a very long time," he said. "Unless...."

She didn't like his use of the word *unless*. But the idea made him sit up, and turn toward her, taking her face in his hands. He often did that before he kissed her, but he didn't kiss her now.

Instead, he peered into her eyes.

"I could take you now. We would be together. We could work together," he said.

And she felt something—a pulling, a change.

She wrenched her face from his grasp and looked away from him.

"No," she said.

"No?" he asked.

"No," she said. "I don't want to live like you do. I've told you that."

"But you are already half in my world," he said. "Come the rest of the way."

"No," she said.

"Then tell your father to stay here," he said.

She shook her head, resisting the urge to scramble off the bed. As long as he didn't peer at her like that again, he wouldn't be able to pull her life from her.

"You made that impossible," she said.

"Me?"

She nodded. "I am an unmarried woman. I am subject to my father's commands. I cannot influence him. So I will move with him."

And she felt—triumphant? Relieved? She wasn't sure. But not unhappy, like she might have expected. Part of her had always hoped this would end.

"You could come to the burial ground," he said.

She imagined it for a half moment—safe inside alabaster chambers, cradled in his arms—and then she shuddered. She would lose herself there. Lose herself, and lose track of time.

She didn't want to say no directly. He would get angry.

Instead, she said, "Is that why you can come here? The burial ground behind the house?"

He nodded. "I belong here."

"And I belong with my family," she said, wondering if that were indeed true. If it were true, why had she been able to see him? If it were true, why had he fallen in love with her?

"Emily, please," he said. "I won't be able to see you again, except fleeting glances at funerals."

"Or deathbeds," she said, wondering if, in some ways, that was what she sat on. A deathbed.

"Or deathbeds," he whispered.

She closed her eyes, not willing to see his anguish. And when she opened them, just a moment later, he was gone.

So was the strange silver light.

And something else—a part of her. A part she had not realized she'd had.

She went to the window and looked out. He was walking among the graves, like he had the first night she had seen him, his robe over his arm, his scythe carried casually in his left hand.

Walking away.

She wondered when she would see him again. How many years? How much time?

Would he again sit on her bed and tell her he loved her? Or would he be angry?

She wasn't sure she ever wanted to find out.

May 24, 1886
The Homestead
Amherst, Massachusetts

Vinnie clutched a pile of poems in one hand. So many about death. Perhaps those were even more shocking than those about love. And the death poems— they weren't typical reminiscences. They were odd, like Emily had been odd, and a bit unfathomable.

Vinnie had even heard Emily speak some of them aloud. Only Vinnie had not realized they were poems at the time.

Like this one, which Emily had spoken late one night, almost unbidden. She looked up from her scratching pen, and smiled sadly at Vinnie. Emily didn't speak the poem exactly as written. She added a bit to make it conversational. But Vinnie remembered it as if it had happened just a week before instead of decades ago.

"Sometimes I think a death-blow is a life-blow to some," Emily said, "who, until they died, did not become alive."

Vinnie had stopped walking by, looked at Emily oddly, and then shrugged, wondering what had provoked that outburst. She still did not know.

Had someone died recently? Had Emily been reacting to something? Or had she simply felt an inspiration?

Except that it felt true, as if something provoked it. Emily often broke into strangely structured speech when provoked, and now Vinnie knew why.

She had been reciting her own poems.

Vinnie wished she could go back, wished she could recapture memories of all of those recitations. Maybe she was; maybe that was why she heard Emily's voice whenever she read a poem. Maybe Emily had spoken them all.

Vinnie clutched the poems against her chest. How could she burn them? They had bits of her sister in them, clinging to them, as if she had not yet died.

March 8, 1860
The Homestead
Amherst, Massachusetts

They were calling her crazy and maybe she was, maybe she was. Certainly she felt wild-eyed and broken, her thoughts swirling in her head. Emily had taken to writing them down, capturing them in bits of paper, and then sewing them into bound booklets like she had done her herbs just a few years before.

At the West Street House, when she used to roam the garden, when she wandered the burial ground.

Emily buried her face in her hands. Her room here in the Homestead was larger than her room in the West Street House. She had a conservatory and a better kitchen. She should have liked it here, in the best house in Amherst.

She should have liked it.

But she didn't.

Her room here overlooked the street. The house was far enough back so that street sounds seemed faint, but through the trees, she could see the horses, watch the carriages, see the *life*.

She let her hands fall. Then she grabbed a sheet of paper, its smoothness soothing to her fingertips. She stared for a moment at the windows, then grabbed her pen and dipped it in ink.

She hadn't thought she would miss him.

I cannot live with you, she wrote. *It would be life, and life is over there behind the shelf the sexton keeps the key to....*

She paused, sighed, and held the pen away from the paper so it wouldn't blot.

She wasn't alive without him. He had taken something from her. Everyone noticed it. They had always thought her strange, but now they feared her, and she wasn't quite sure why.

She hid away from them, mostly because she didn't want to see the fear in their eyes.

She wrote, *I could not die with you.*

Was she writing him a letter? And if so, where would she leave it? Did she truly want him to find it, to know she missed him?

Nor could I rise with you, because your face would put out Jesus's....

Her hand trembled as she wrote.

They'd judge us—how? For you served Heaven, you know, or sought to. I could not.

No one dared see these. Not him, not anyone. Think of what they would say. Think of what they would do to her, even in this enlightened time.

She shuddered, feeling the temptation to go to him. But she could not. She dared not.

So we must keep apart, she wrote to him. She *was* writing to him now. She had known that, but she finally acknowledged it. *You there, I here, with just the door ajar....*

The door ajar. That was what the others felt. She straddled the world between, half her life there, half here. She hadn't fled him quickly enough.

She hadn't known what he would cost her, what she had chosen. Then, five years ago, she had tried to go back to a normal life, not realizing it was too late.

So she lived in this strange half-world, neither here nor there, not willing to cross the threshold into his life—and Eternity, not able to fully live in hers.

She hadn't expected this, and she had no idea how to live with it.

Except to scrawl the maddening thoughts. Except to try to quell the feeling of panic, always rising inside.

Her pen, her paper. Her silence. She had nothing else left.

April 20, 1862
Worcester, Massachusetts

The envelope itself looked a bit odd, the handwriting tiny, the edges a bit too thick. That Higginson noticed it was odd too, considering the volume of mail he got lately. He had published an essay titled "A Letter to a Young Contributor" in the *Atlantic Monthly*, hoping to slow down the volume of unsolicited submissions the magazine got as the war got underway. Instead, his essay increased them. And worse, they were all addressed to him.

Only the most select made it to his study in Worcester. Later he would say he added the thick envelope because he had known it carried something marvelous, but at the time, he had taken it only because it struck him as unusual.

He sat in his leather-backed chair, a mound of manuscripts on one side, and his own writing paper on the other. Books surrounded him. He didn't keep newspapers in his study, preferring they remain in the parlor. The news since Lincoln's inaugural a year before had been ugly at best, and Higginson wanted to keep horror out of his study.

He had a hunch it would enter his life all too soon.

He slit the envelope with his letter opener, careful not to disturb the papers inside. A second envelope tumbled out, followed by five sheets of paper—four poems and an unsigned letter. He opened that envelope first, only to find a card inside with the name Emily Dickinson printed upon it in pencil. The five pages had been written in pen.

Intrigued, he started with the letter:

Mr Higginson,

Are you too deeply occupied to say if my Verse
is alive?
The Mind is so near itself—it cannot see,
distinctly—and I have none to ask—
Should you think it breathed—and had
you the leisure to tell me, I should feel quick gratitude—
If I make the mistake—that you dared to tell me—
would give me sincerer honor—toward you—
I enclose my name—asking you, if you please—
Sir—to tell me what is true?
That you will not betray me—it is needless to ask—
since Honor is its own pawn—

The breathless style startled him and it carried over to the poems, all untitled. Of course the verse lived; he had never seen such life in poetry, and he had read a lot. An untamed life, that reflected the writer more than any other poems he had ever read, as if the writer put herself on the page without regard to convention, or even to a reader.

He reread all of the documents before answering Miss Dickinson. Her verse was alive, her words breathed. But the grammatical errors grated on him. He tapped the tip of his pen against his teeth. He had somehow to tell her that she wasn't yet ready for publication without destroying the spirit that crackled out of the poetry.

Finally he decided he would operate on the poems himself, and she would be able to learn from his surgery. He meticulously copied what she had done, then set about to repair it.

October 5, 1883
The Evergreens
Amherst, Massachusetts

It was a mistake, Emily knew it was a mistake, but she couldn't stop herself, she didn't dare stop herself, didn't dare *think* about any of it as she clung to Vinnie's arm and stepped outside the house. The fresh evening air seemed a mockery— next door, right next door, little Gilbert was dying, didn't the Gods know that?

Of course they did; they had ordered it, and because they had ordered it, she cursed them for reveling in the death of children.

She adored Gib, her brother's youngest child, born late. Witty and funny and oh, so alive, he made her feel like a child again. Certainly she hadn't laughed so hard in the years before he learned to speak—maybe she hadn't laughed at all.

She loved him, her heart's child, and now typhoid was taking him, and she couldn't stay away, even though she knew she should, even though she tried.

She had picked the right moment to flee her own mother's bedside, and her father's too. Vinnie had to tend the dying, because Emily could not, frightened as she was of ever seeing *him* again.

But she could not flee Gib's bedside and forgive herself. Sometimes love made harsh demands, and this was one.

She walked across the yard into a house as outwardly familiar as her own. Huge, built in the style of an Italian villa, the Evergreens housed the other Dickinsons, the ones who ran her life—her brother Austin, his wife Sue, and their three beautiful children.

That Austin had all but abandoned Sue few knew except Emily. She didn't approve of Austin's mistress, Mabel Loomis Todd, but Emily didn't dare disapprove either, not after the way she had lost herself all those years ago. Austin was here tonight, but Miss Todd was not, and Emily was grateful for that. Even though she knew Miss Todd frequented Emily's home, Emily had not seen her and preferred to pretend that Miss Todd herself was little more than a ghost.

Vinnie put a hand over Emily's as they walked up the steps into the Evergreens. Emily had not been inside in fifteen years, seeing it only from the windows of the Homestead. Her heart pounded as if she had walked a thousand miles, and the smell—the smell nearly turned her stomach.

It was a sick house, reeking of camphor and vomit and despair.

But she continued forward, leaning on Vinnie a bit too much, walking up the stairs to Gib's bedchamber, the smells growing stronger, harsher, more insistent.

Vinnie, bless her, did not say a word. When they reached the door, Emily let out a sigh of relief. *He* was not there. Gib would not die this night.

The boy looked small in his bed, too thin for an eight-year-old, too frail to be the vital child Emily so adored. Sue—grown matronly in middle age—saw Emily and hugged her so tightly that Emily couldn't catch her breath. Austin peered at her from his post near the bureau.

"You're too frail," Austin said. "We don't need you ill as well."

Emily glared at him, and Austin looked away, as everyone did when she gave them her gimlet eye. Then she sat beside Gib and took his hand.

His eyes opened for a brief moment and he saw her. "Aunt Emily," he breathed, his voice raspy and congested.

"Gib," she said, unable to find words for the first time in her life.

His skin was too hot, his eyes glistened with fever. He turned away from her, but kept his hand clamped around hers. Sue placed wet cloths on his forehead, and Austin fretted about feeding the child.

But Emily simply held his dry little hand, hoping he would look at her again. He did not.

Instead, there was an emptiness in the room. She looked up, the hair on the back of her neck rising. She and Gib were momentarily alone. Sue had gone for more cloths, Austin for water or perhaps just to escape, Vinnie to find camphor to ease Gib's increasingly labored breathing.

The light suddenly turned silver, and Emily inwardly cursed. She had not made her escape.

He had come, and he would see her, an old woman, losing a child of her heart. She didn't look up. Instead she wrapped her free hand around Gib's.

"Don't take him," she said. "Please don't take him."

"You know I can't do that." His voice was as she remembered, only more musical, deep and filled with warmth. "I have missed you, Emily, more than I could ever express."

"Don't." She brought her head up, and her gaze met his.

Damnation, he was still beautiful. His cowl was down, his scythe against the wall. He looked like he had moved in, and despite that, despite the horror of it, she felt his pull even now. He reached out to touch her and she leaned away.

"This is about Gib, not me," she said. "Don't take him."

"I must," he said. He didn't sound sorrowful. He didn't know Gib. She did.

"Take me instead," she said. "My life for his."

He shook his head. "You're already half mine, Emily," he said. "It's not a fair trade. Is there another life you would give for his?"

Her heart chilled. He would have her trade someone else's life for Gib's? What kind of bargain was that?

"Take me, *please*," she said. "You have always wanted me."

He nodded. "And I still do. I love you, Emily."

She knew that; she also knew that she had loved him once, and feared him too. She didn't fear him now. All she feared was his power.

"So you have what you want," she said. "Leave Gib. Let him grow up."

He looked at his hands as if they were not his. Then he sighed. "I cannot, Emily. His soul is incandescent. Pure."

She knew his next words, but she didn't want to hear him say them. "And mine is not."

"I'm sorry," he whispered. "But you can come with us."

"No," she said. "*No.*"

He touched Gib, and Gib froze—froze!—the heat leaving his body.

"*No,*" she said again. "No!"

And then they were both gone—he and Gib, the scythe, everything—leaving only a frail shell behind.

Everyone came back into the room as if they had been summoned, Sue leading, tears on her dear familiar face, Austin looking ancient and horrible, and Vinnie, Vinnie, hands clasped to her chest.

They crowded the body and Emily staggered away, mouth tasting of paper, eyes dry, head aching.

"Take me home," she said to Vinnie. "Please."

Emily had to go home now, taking her fragile, ragged, worthless little soul. If she hadn't had a fruitless romance with *him*, if she hadn't wasted all of that time, she still would have seen him here, and she could have bargained with him, she could have given him her soul in place of Gib's and it would not have been worthless. Gib would have lived, and so would she.

But *he* had cheated her of that. He had known, and he had cheated her, because he claimed he loved her.

Could one such as that love?

She didn't know. She didn't want to think of it. Not now, and maybe not ever.

May 24, 1886
The Homestead
Amherst, Massachusetts

Twilight was falling as Vinnie picked up the last pile of poems. She had just lit Emily's favorite lamp, giving the room a brief scent of kerosene and burned wick.

Vinnie's hands shook. She was exhausted, but unwilling to quit. The poems—ah, the poems—they were Emily, and more than Emily. They were about her life too.

There's been a death in the opposite house, began one, and Vinnie set it aside. She could not read that. It was about Gib. There were a number about Gib, some even calling him by name.

Gib's death had destroyed Emily. From that moment forward, she had been ill, although most did not know it. She continued her letters and, clearly, her poetry, but little else, her eyes hollow, her expression always a little lost.

Not with a club the heart is broken, Emily whispered, *nor with a stone. A whip so small you could not see it....*

Like a poem, Vinnie thought. Like a poem.

"I can't do it, Em," she whispered as if her sister were still here. For all she knew, her sister was alive in the poetry, haunting the room like a restless ghost. "I can't do it."

Burning the poems would be like losing Emily all over again. And storing them would be wrong too, because Austin or his daughter Mattie might burn them, following Emily's wishes.

Vinnie would burn the papers, burn the letters. She would do that much. But the poems were alive, like her sister had been, and she could not destroy them.

Finally, Emily had to step out of her room and let the world see her as Vinnie had seen her, all those years ago—vibrant and witty and filled with an astonishing love.

May 15, 1886
The Homestead
Amherst, Massachusetts

He came like she knew he would, his face filled with triumph. Emily was too weak to fight him. She couldn't get out of bed, she couldn't even open her eyes, yet she could see him, sitting on the edge of the bed, his hand gripping hers.

"Are you ready to join me, Emily?" he asked, not trying to disguise the joy in his voice.

"No," she said. "I will never join you."

"You have no choice," he said. "I take everyone."

"But you do not keep them," she said. "You taught me all those years ago how to defeat you. When the memory is gone, the soul goes too. After Vinnie, after Austin, after Mattie, no one will remember me."

"Except me," he said.

"And you do not count," she said, "because you remember everyone you touched."

His eyes widened just a little. "You hate me, Em?"

"For Gib," she said. "I'll never forgive you for Gib."

"Never is a long time," he said.

"But do not fear," she said. "I have escaped Eternity."

"Would it be so bad, Emily, spending forever with me?" he asked.

"Yes," she said. "It would."

"You do not mean it," he said as he took what was left of her soul. She felt a momentary relief, a respite from pain she hadn't realized she had, and then a brief incandescent sense of joy.

Only a few more years and they would go quickly. Vinnie would see to it. Nothing of Emily would remain, nothing except a name carved into a stone above an old and sunken grave—and someday, not even that.

She had won. God help her, she had finally won.

May 15, 1892
Cambridge, Massachusetts

Higginson had the dream again. He used to dream of that clearing in Florida, filled with bodies laid out symmetrically. But ever since he turned in his edited version of *The Poems of Emily Dickinson* to the publisher, this dream had supplanted the other.

Emily, as he had first seen her, red hair parted, white dress, beseeching him not to betray her. *Honor me*, she would say, her eyes silver and terrifying. *Honor me.*

And he would say, *I am. I am making your work known.*

Then she would raise her arms, like a banshee from Irish lore, and screech, and as she screeched, the hooded figure would rise behind her and clasp his arms around her, dragging her to the clearing and all those dead men….

And Higginson would wake, heart pounding, breath coming in rapid gasps.

This morning, after the dream, he threw on his dressing gown and made his way to his study. He knew why he had had the dream this time. Another volume of *The Poems by Emily Dickinson* had arrived with a note that this was the seventh edition.

Seven. And more to come. He and Mabel Loomis Todd had barely touched the thousand manuscripts Miss Dickinson had left. He admitted to no one how surprised he was; he had thought her words too strange for the reading public, her gift too rare.

But they adored it, some, he thought, in part to the surgery he had felt it necessary to perform, ridding it of her excessive dashes and her breathless punctuation. But still, the essence of her lived.

Are you too deeply occupied to say if my Verse is alive? she had written him in that very first letter.

And now he could answer her truthfully: her verse was more alive than ever. *She* was more alive than ever.

So why had the first sight of the seventh edition filled him with such horror?

He picked it up and thumbed through it—stopping suddenly at unfamiliar words. He did not recall editing this poem.

He eased into his favorite chair, book in hand, and read:

> *Because I could not stop for Death,*
> *He kindly stopped for me;*
> *The carriage held but just ourselves*
> *And Immortality.*

There was no despair mentioned in the poem, and yet he felt it, like he felt that banshee scream.

What had she written to him once, when she mentioned his books about the War?

My wars are laid away in books.

Yes. Yes they were.

He closed the volume, determined to never open it again.

The Happiest Hell on Earth

By

John Skipp & Cody Goodfellow

May 5, 1972
To: Spec. Agent R. Stanley
Federal Bureau of Investigation

As you probably know, Prisoner #0003 has died, after 37 years in solitary confinement for his role in the Animal Wars. He was the last and longest-held of the original conspirators, the rest having either been executed or paroled to their new homeland in Florida when Nixon and Governor Gator signed the Animal Liberation treaty last year.

That he resisted extradition to Moreauvia while refusing to disavow his crimes was no reflection on his daily conduct. He was a model prisoner until the day he leapt from his window in the VIP block, having torn the bars out with his trunk, in a display of strength we would never have expected, given his age. He never had any contact with the outside world, but even after his movie was banned and the UN declared him a war criminal, the elephant-man still got a lot of fan mail from the forty-eight "two-legged" states.

Because Mr. Hoover always took such a special interest in his case, we believe #0003 was just waiting for the death of your illustrious Director: not only to end his own life, but to reveal the enclosed manuscript, which we found neatly stacked upon his cot. The fact that he waited *only one day* after Mr. Hoover's death lends credence to this interpretation.

I truly shudder to think of the effect this will have on the public, if any of it is proven true, but I earnestly hope that it will be buried no longer. This poor, divided nation deserves to know why so many millions of Americans still live in the trees, and who is truly responsible.

That is why I have also forwarded copies to Ben Bradlee, Jack Anderson, Jann Wenner, William F. Buckley, and people at several other media outlets.

Let it be known: I am a Republican and a patriot, and am prepared to face all consequences. I do this not to bring our country down, but to restore it to its greatness.

Good luck, God bless America, and apologies for the inconvenience.

Sincerely,
From: Warden R. Clampett
Texarkana Federal Prison

DOCUMENT A
PART ONE: ON THE ISLAND OF LOST SOULS

The rosy dawn paints the gray sands. The bull-men in their white shrouds wait, snorting, pawing. Disturbed by something on the wind.

The Master stands in the launch, arms at his sides like a conductor at rest. Behind me, the jungle clenches like a green fist, flexing its claws. They have all come to see the return of the Other with the Whip, and what he has brought with him.

M'ling crouches in the bow, pointed ears back to bask in the sea breeze on his black face. The less favored beasts bend to their oars, and Montgomery sneaks a nip from a flask, as he answers the Master's questions. Loaded to the gunwales with supplies and fresh specimens—a puma, a llama, six hutches of rabbits, and a pack of excited staghounds.

But all eyes are hooked on the sinking lifeboat towed behind the launch, and the solitary creature sitting in it.

What kind of animal would be so dangerous that the Doctor would not have it in the launch?

From the crown of a palm tree, Virgil the monkey-man howls. "A Five-Man! A Five-Man, like me!"

By slow, painful turns, the launch creeps into the cut in the shore. The bull-men bow to the Master and the Other as they unload the cages and crates. I take up the ledger and, with a quill pen in my trunk, make a tally of the goods.

The strange man climbs awkwardly out of his lifeboat and wallows up onto the beach.

Claws lose their purchase on boxes and drop them in the surf. All eyes follow the Stranger as he approaches the Master. Without fear, without bowing his head.

He was on a schooner touring the Galapagos Islands that got wrecked in a storm. It was nothing less than a miracle that Montgomery's chartered tramp steamer happened upon him in his lifeboat. The Captain put the Stranger off with Montgomery after he came between poor M'ling and the vicious, bullying crew. "Someone is sure to come looking for me...."

"Here," the Master says, "they are unlikely to find you."

The Stranger asks for a radio, and is told we have none. The steamer puts in only thrice a year, and the island is well off the shipping lanes. Though uninvited, he is to be our guest.

The Stranger looks from the bull-men to M'ling to the Ape Man to me, and shows his blunt teeth, sharp tongue. His eyes burn us. He offers to pay for his lodging, and to make himself useful however he can.

Taller than the Other, younger than the Master, skin burned red and blistered. Dark hair covers his weak chin, but he walks erect, in tight circles when nowhere else to go. He was never an animal. Perhaps he was never a child.

The Stranger puts a stick of paper in his soft mouth. Fire sprouts from his hand and sets the stick alight. We gasp. He has fire in his hands, and smoke spills from his thin lips. Perhaps he is a machine.

The Master asks of his education. "We are both scientists, and this is a biological station, of a sort."

Still chewing us with his eyes, the Stranger says, "I have some experience with running complex operations, and I'm a quick study. I was raised on a farm, and I drove an ambulance in the War ... after the Armistice was signed. I'm not afraid of a little blood."

"Our work here is of great import, but of too delicate a nature to take you into our confidence, just yet."

"I'm in your hands, Dr. Moreau," the Stranger says.

We have peace and order on our island. The Master tells us it is not so in the wider world. We are humble before the Law. Until he comes among us, we can dream of no other life.

The Master leaves the Stranger in an outer apartment of the compound, and locks the inner door to the courtyard. He summons me to attend to his initial examination of the new specimens.

He needs me. The Other drinks poison to make his mind weak and his notes are sloppy, and though my blunt forelimbs are clumsy, my trunk can do the fine work, even sometimes with the Knife, and the Master says I have an extraordinary head for figures. I have seen pictures of my ancestors, of the clay from which the Master made me. I am stunted, a dwarf. The House of Pain made me small, but bright.

I do not carry a whip or a gun, but the Master gave me a blue serge suit like his, and I work with him. The others in the compound must wear white. They are proud of their status but hate the white, which hides no dirt. The beasts in the ravine despise me, for though many of them have better hands and truer voices, I live in the House of Pain. I was made to teach them to speak and to read, but they have come as far as the Knife and the Needle can take them. To learn more only teaches them that they are still beasts.

The Stranger hunts us.

While the Master begins to remake the puma with Montgomery, the Stranger leaves his apartment and ambles into the jungle. He has shaved the fur from his face, but kept a tiny strip of hair just above his lips. It makes him look less like an animal, and yet more dangerous.

I cannot keep up with his long-legged strides without giving myself away, but he stops and sits beside the creek and blows smoke into the air.

The secret of fire is not in making it, but making it work. The burning in his head comes out on the paper in his lap. With swift stabs and slashes of the pencil, his fine fingers make a window in the paper. The creek and the canebrake beyond are trapped in it; and then, as if summoned, Darius skulks out of the shadows, eyes greenly flashing.

Most of them cannot recall or even speak the names I gave them, but this is of little import to me. Was it not Adam's first task to name the beasts of the field? Even if they failed this simple test, I did not fail mine.

Darius stoops on all fours to slurp water from the creek. He knows no shame. Time and again, the Master has ripped out his claws, but they always grow back. Even his flesh hates the Law. His tawny flanks heave with panting. The faded spots on his piebald hide flush. His muzzle and paws are speckled with red.

Fear. I would trumpet and run on all fours, so strong is my terror. But the Stranger only says, "Hello," and draws the leopard man in the depth of his sin.

With a coughing growl, Darius leaps the creek and coils, ready to pounce. The Stranger stands erect and stares Darius down with his redly flashing eyes.

The leopard man runs away into the green jungle. The Stranger shakes his head and turns to a fresh page. Then he turns on me.

"Hello, little fellow. You're a shy one, aren't you? Well, you needn't be frightened of me. Here...." His teeth flash, but not in threat. He reaches into his pocket and holds out a handful of peanuts.

I trample out of my hiding place. My ears flap and my trunk unfurls in a vulgar display of threat, but the Stranger barks until he coughs and spits on the ground. "You really are some sort of a beast-man, aren't you? Not a hoodoo or a gaff, at all. Now, what would be a good name for you...?"

"I have a name," I tell him. I try to make my voice large. It cracks and he utters his strange bark again, like the hyena-swine's mating call.

My trunk reaches out to snort up a nut. "My name...." My remade throat closes, my tongue twists, spitting shells. "Diogenes."

The Stranger's pencil carves a bloated, droopy ellipse, with a wilted triangle on either side, and a lazy S dangling from its belly. Then two smaller circles beneath it, and short, stubby rectangular limbs. The eyes are bigger than mine, the humors out of balance to drive this paper Diogenes mad with glee. My own eyes are small and weak and sad.

He shakes his head again. "I can't do justice to you. Nobody could believe it, nobody would fall in love with it. But you're real enough, aren't you, little fellow? D'you know any tricks?"

My clumsy hands reach out for the book. He turns it around and shows it to me. I take his pencil in my trunk and write my name under his picture.

Cradling it in my hands, I turn the pages with my trunk. He has seen many of us. The hyena-swine creeps up on a rabbit hutch. A wolf woman falls upon a swine man and destroys his crude cane-stick hut. The pink homunculi at play in the undergrowth. A headless rabbit sprawls in the grass, bejeweled with flies. The leopard man slakes his thirst after a murder. "He has broken the Law," I grunt.

Behind the picture of Darius, I find sketches of other beast men, with no claws or teeth—soft, like the homunculi, but with gloves and short pants. "It's not ... a good likeness ... of a rabbit."

He barks again, but does not smile. "Animals are no fit judges of artwork," he says. "And it's a mouse."

"I've read Homer and Aesop ... in the orig ... original Greek ... and Latin." There are more sketches of this curious animal-baby, on the corner of each page. When the pages slip from my blunt thumbnail, the little rodent dances like a little live thing.

"That ... no, don't look at that." He snaps the book away and tears the page out, balls it up and puts it in his mouth. His red face dims almost purple. He chokes it down. "That's over and gone. They stole it from me, but they won't take anything from me again." He sucks in fire and blows out smoke, and slowly grows calm again. "How does he do it, Diogenes? You're a sharp one. You can tell Uncle Wilbur."

I don't know what he means. He offers me more peanuts, but I know not to take them. His eyes are like whips.

"You're a true friend to your Master, aren't you? Well, never mind. I'll find out for myself."

We go back to the compound. The Stranger locks himself in his apartment and says he must sleep, but he does not sleep. From lying in his hammock staring at Aesop's Fables—what kind of man cannot read Greek?—to pacing the room until it is filled with smoke, he wastes the day. I watch through the outer window that looks on the ocean, but I cannot imagine what disturbs him. He has the key to his cage.

Inside, the puma cries out. Her cries send him pacing faster. She is a long way yet from being born.

M'ling brings him his supper. The Stranger hides his book of drawings. Montgomery comes in and he and the Stranger share a glass of poison. He warns the Stranger to be careful in his wandering, for the island is dangerous, then leaves by the inner courtyard door, but he forgets to lock it.

The poison overtakes the Stranger. He has bad dreams. Crying out in echo of the unmade puma, he says, "No, Father, don't," and covers his head. This strange creature is no stranger to the Whip.

In the morning, his hammock is soiled. M'ling sniffs at the stain and the Stranger's discarded rags and says he has marked his place.

The newborn woman cries out. The Stranger pokes at his breakfast for a while, then goes through the door into the compound. Slow on my flat feet, I follow.

The dogs snarl and bark. The Stranger runs them to the span of their leashes, then ducks into the open back door of the House of Pain.

Dark inside. Hotter than outside. Clean. White porcelain and polished steel. Chains. And the new woman on the table. Still red and wet and weeping, mewling lost in the throes of rebirth.

The Master shouts, takes him by the arm and hurls him from the room into the courtyard, then drives him back to his apartment and slams the door.

The Other is shamefaced. The Master almost whips him. "This uninvited guest will be our undoing. His meddling could ruin the work of a lifetime!"

"He doesn't know the score," hisses Montgomery, "but he wants to. Too eager by half, says I. In fact, when I riddle upon it, I wonder if his coming here was an accident, after all."

"That is my principal fear. He must be taken into our confidence or dealt with, but I can't yet spare the time."

Montgomery chuckles. "If he's as fine a specimen as you seem to think, perhaps you could turn his presence here to the good—"

The Master looms over the Other. The puma's blood on his smock is the only color on his white marble face. "This Wilbur Dixon is a singular creature, but imagine his blood in their bodies. No, they would walk erect and speak, but I doubt they could be less human." The Master sees me watching, and orders me to find the Stranger.

He has left his apartment. He races, but I can follow the trail of his smoke through the trees.

Someone else stalks us. I scent Darius' bitter musk on the rank morning heat. The Stranger can smell nothing but his own smoke. He is helpless before the hunched gray shape that drops out of a tree before him.

I wheeze with relief. The monkey man bows and presents his fingers for counting. Amused, the Stranger returns the gesture, but he can make no sense of Virgil's chattering.

"You poor creature! You were a spider monkey, weren't you?"

"I am a man, like you, yes yes. We talk big thinks, yes yes?" Virgil prances and chatters around the Stranger, who makes the sound he calls laughter, and throws him nuts.

"What has that monster done to your tail?"

Angry Virgil tries to stand erect and puff out his chest. "I am a man like you! The Master made me, good Virgil, yes yes, a man!"

The Stranger puts a hand on Virgil's head and strokes his gray fur. "You had a tail once. He's taken all of your God-given gifts, and for what? This Moreau is a butcher, and the worst sort of villain. Someone should make him pay for his crimes against you."

"Moreau a butcher, yes no," Virgil chatters. "His is the hand that wounds! His is the hand that heals!"

"Where are the rest of you?" the Stranger asks. "How many orphans are there?"

Virgil turns and scampers down the trail. "I will take you to them, yes yes. You must learn the Law."

The Stranger blunders through the canebreak after Virgil and emerges on the yellow waste. Sulfur and steam rise from the hot springs, masking the mouth of the ravine. I wait for them to disappear into the mist, when something rakes my back with claws of fire.

I forget myself, and trumpet wordless terror. My blood flows. I try to turn over, but I am pinned. I have no gun, no whip. I have never had tusks. I cannot even call for the Master.

Darius sinks his teeth into my tough hide and flays my scalp, then flies away. The Stranger brandishes a bloody rock, then throws it at the leopard man. He strikes him on the temple and sends him howling into a thorny thicket.

"You're safe now, little friend." He reaches out for my trunk, and lifts me up.

He goes into the ravine.

The stone walls draw close. They come out of their huts of thorns and palm fronds in the cracks of the rock to show fangs and claws and half-made hands. I count heads. Sixty-two. All but M'ling and Darius are here.

Pan lowers his goatish head to show his curling horns, fondles himself and strikes the rock with his hooves. The swine-folk hoot and the wolves growl, the dog-man grovels and licks the Stranger's boots.

A man walks among them, unarmed. He tests the Law. It is too much.

He shows no fear. The stink from him is not like an animal's fear. I doubt anyone but me can smell it. It is the stink of a deeper fear, buried under a mountain of will.

The gray-haired oldest one limps from his hovel and lifts himself upright on his staff. I call him Solon, for he speaks only the Law. His shaggy pelt hides his blind eyes, toothless mouth. "If it is a man, then let him say the Law!"

"The Law of the Jungle is the only law I see here," says the Stranger. "I see only animals stripped of their true nature and their gifts, and cast adrift."

The beast men roar and jeer. "Not to walk on all fours—that is the Law! Are we not men?"

"Not to spill blood—*that* is the Law! Are we not men?"

"Not to suck drink—*that* is the Law! Are we not men?"

The Stranger rages. "No, you are *not*! Not to do those things is not to be an animal, but has he taught you what it is to be a man?"

He takes out a little silver tool and blows into it. The single, piercing note traps every beast in the ravine. None of them have ever heard music.

He begins to play the swooning, swaying notes of a familiar tune—Saint-Saens's *Danse Macabre*, I know it from the Master's phonograph collection. Heads bobbing, eyes glazed, they become less than beasts, but Virgil knows at once what music is for.

Bobbing his furry head to the woozy melody, he prances in circles around the Stranger in uncanny imitation of the Stranger's stiff, inhibited gait. When he runs up the Stranger's back to snatch his hat, the Stranger does not punish him, but only quickens the whirling, maddening tune.

Virgil leaps to the ground and dances on his hands, holding the hat in place on his hindquarters, covering the stump of his tail. Then, flipping over and miming crapping into the hat, he offers it back.

The Stranger drops his harmonica and again makes that strange, bloodcurdling bark. He slaps his palms together to make a thunderous sound that drives the beasts back into their burrows. But then his brow darkens, and he looks angry. "Your Master never taught you to laugh?"

Silence, but a riot of scent. In the dim cave shadows, his eyes flash red.

Solon bellows, "His is the hand that wounds—"

The Stranger utters that frightening bark again. "Ask yourselves, if you are really men, what has he done for you? Your master, your creator, who rules by fear and pain, who left you to rot in sin and filth: what do you owe him?" He wipes his brow. The beasts are too captivated to rip him apart. It seems he must do it himself. His eyes shine, and stream down his face. "In the place I come from, you would all be celebrated for your gifts. Instead of a Master who whips and shuns you, you would have a loving father who gives you work and a purpose. And there would be no damnable House of Pain!"

Only a few of them understand his words, but then Virgil takes up a new chant. "No Pain! No pain!"

The others cannot even parrot his words, but they roar and stamp and crush their own huts in perfect imitation of his fury. My own trunk is lifted in the chorus.

We are so loud that none sees the dogs until they fall upon us.

The Master has returned. He holds the barking dogs to heel, but they have torn the hyena-swine's filthy white tunic. Montgomery cracks his whip over our heads.

A hairless pink sloth-child I call Claudius scurries up the Stranger's leg. He scoops it up and cradles it to his chest to shield it from the dogs.

Moreau holds out the Stranger's sketchbook. The drawing of Darius. "This one has broken the Law! We will have him."

"None escape! None escape!" The beasts chant.

"Not to spill blood—*that* is the Law!"

"That is your Law," the Stranger shouts, "but why should it be theirs? You give them only pain and turn them loose in the jungle, and grant them only enough sense to recognize that their creator has forsaken them!"

"You misunderstand my aim," the Master says, in a lower tone. "Please come back to the compound. I would rather have you know all than—"

"The Master is not a god. He is a man like all of you, and yes, an animal, too! He is not above the Law, is he? He and his lackey are only men, and they are only two, while you are many—"

"For God's sake, man, shut up!" the Other cracks his whip at the Stranger, who does not cower, but lunges at Montgomery, roaring, "Don't you dare!" and clouts him across the face.

The Master hurls the fire of death into the sky. Its thunderclap sends all of us down on all fours. "Mr. Dixon, we came here to save you from harm. But you have done us a mortal blow. Come with us now, before something transpires that cannot be undone."

The Stranger refuses to leave with the Master. Some of us growl and circle the arguing men, but the rest stand dumb, or cling to the earth as if it's trying to shake them off. If either of them had eyes to see, they could tell now who is the most human among us.

"If it will ease your suspicions," the Master says, and turns over his pistol. Montgomery refuses to disarm, and lewdly slurps from his flask. "Where's the leopard man?"

"He attacked your poor pachyderm houseboy, when you sent him to spy on me. He could be anywhere."

"Mr. Dixon, if you please." Bowing to the Stranger, he turns and walks down the ravine. The Other goes backwards after him with his pistol out before him. "Remember who's the Master here, you rum bastards."

The Other steps on the paw of the cringing hyena-swine. It whines and strikes him with its gnarled claw-hoof. He shoots it through the head.

The thunder is a long time falling away into silence.

"You rash idiot!" The Master takes off his straw hat. "What a terrible waste..."

"We all know who is the master here, Mr. Montgomery," says the Stranger. Gently, he sets down the sloth-child and follows the men. And I go with them.

The Master stitches my wounded scalp and sends me to sleep. Night falls, and the jungle is loud. The beast men claw at trees and stalk prey, battle, and breed in the dark. The Law is broken, and they want us to hear it.

The Master and the Stranger retire to the library to drink poison and talk. For a long time, the Master explains his great work, his failures and his triumphs. His dashed hopes and determination to go on. With fierce pride, he defends his studies. How the necessary pain of rebirth wipes away the animal memory, leaving a blank slate upon which to build a man. How vivisection and blood and tissue transplants led the way to this great mission, to uplift the animal kingdom into the brotherhood of man.

If only the Stranger could listen.

"Dr. Moreau, this place is an abomination. I beg you to reconsider my offer."

"Even if it were so simple, Mr. Dixon, I could never walk away from this place, and you could never take it over. I fully recognize the ethical burden of my undertaking, but it is only in the name of science—"

"Science! Like Communism, the rationale for all modern inhumanity. Neither men nor animals should be tortured as you do."

"To rear a child, one must flay away that which is animal, no? To be born is painful, and none of us asked for it. They are born anew, but they must be taught, like any new human. And my hand is not quick enough, sadly, to give them the gift of true humanity."

"You're a strange sort of parent, to turn your babes out into the wilderness! You gave up on them, but who has failed? Hard work and a little cleanliness, that's what's wanted here! Without constant hard work, discipline, and a little church, what men won't backslide into savagery?"

The Stranger fills his glass and drinks it. He puts a paper stick in his mouth and lets the smoke out of his head.

"My coming here was not entirely an accident," he says. "I believe it was destiny. You've had your say. Now listen to me.

"I was born in Chicago, but grew up on an apple farm in Kansas. My father ... was a hardworking man, and he expected us to chip in. There was plenty of work for decent folks, but to make your way in the world, you had to have an idea. And you'd still have to work yourself half to death, just to end up with something worthwhile.

"But if you have a dream, then everyone and his brother is out to crush you. To steal your dream or just rip it to shreds and leave nothing behind. Believe me, Doctor, I know what it's like to have your dreams taken away."

He fills his glass again. "I had a dream, not so different from yours, in essence. I wanted to create life, and inspire wonder. I thought I could do it with films. I don't suppose you know, but I'm somewhat well known in America as an animator."

The Master and the Other share a look. Neither of them knows what it means.

"I make films using a series of drawings to simulate motion, life, emotion. We made the first cartoon with a full sound track. Our short cartoons were popular ... so popular, in fact, that none of the studios would distribute them without taking away ownership of my most beloved character. They called my work primitive trash, but what they couldn't buy or bully away from me, they simply stole. And they got the courts to back them up.

"Now, when I first landed on your island, I was shocked by what I saw, and horrified by your callous treatment of your creations. But when I look at these miserable, flea-bitten creatures, I feel certain that some good may still come of them. Their lives need not be nasty, brutish, and short."

The Master politely says, "I do not take your meaning, sir."

The Other barges in and cackles. He is very sick. "He's making you an offer, Master! He wants to buy your sideshow."

The Stranger sniffs. He is also sick. "Hollywood is not a sideshow, Montgomery. You've clearly abandoned their education. Consider it an extension of your experiment, if you will—"

"I think you should take him up on it, Guv." The Other limbers up his whip. "They're at the gate, rarin' to go, bags packed."

The beasts have not forgotten all of the Master's lessons. The walls of the compound are on fire.

"See what you've done!" the Master shoves the Stranger out onto the porch to see the flames and hear the cries of the beast-men. "Before you came, they were content—"

"You brought this on yourself, Doctor. I hope they will be more merciful to you than you were to them."

"Don't forget this one, Dixon." The door to the laboratory flies open and the red woman splashes into the room.

The Master has only begun to feed her the Needle and human blood—His blood—to change her mind. The Knife, however, has been busy. The freshly sculpted digits of her clawless paws drive her mad with agony. The cracked and reset pelvis betrays her when she tries to run on all fours.

But her broken mind and body are sound enough to choose between the two masters before her.

She pounces on Dr. Moreau.

Dixon shoots her in the flank. His hand shakes. He aims at the Master's heart, and then his hand falls.

A rock smashes the window behind Montgomery, who looks the room over once and shouts, "Damn it all," then flees.

With no claws, the puma-woman bats pitifully at the Master, but her teeth are still sharp. Her mouth closes on his forearm and snaps the bones. He howls for Montgomery.

She goes for his throat.

The Stranger closes his eyes and shoots. The red woman twirls in the air and trips on her insides, shrieks, and dies.

Without a word, the Stranger goes outside.

I come out from my hiding place. The Master orders me to leave him, and go to the surgery.

"Get all the alcohol … and douse my journals. My work must not fall into the wrong hands. And this man—"

"Please … Master…." Smoke pours in the windows. I will not need to fuel the fire. I try to move the Doctor, but he is too large, and he is ready to die.

"Go, Diogenes. You were a faithful assistant … and a good man."

The burning roof crashes through the room. I turn and run on all fours.

Outside, the wall has collapsed, and the beasts rampage through the burning house, hair on fire, mad with poison and the end of the Law. I can barely carry my own head, but I must tear off my blue serge suit, or I will meet the same fate as Mr. Montgomery, the Other with the Whip. Down on the beach, between the launches, they crowd round his body to get at the scraps.

I hide in the icehouse, beneath a pile of cadavers. The celebration goes on until dawn, when there is nothing left unburned.

I come out from my hiding place to wade through ashes. The beasts are gathered on the beach. In their midst, Wilbur Dixon stands with a gun in his hand. He hasn't enough bullets to kill them all, and they are far beneath even the reasoning of a loaded gun.

"I promised you a new life, without pain, with hope and the promise of becoming true men. I do not lie."

He points the gun at the sky and fires. A red flower of fire blooms and fades in the rosy dawn light.

He sets fire to a stick and blows out smoke. The beasts are captivated by this, but only for so long. They begin to close in on him. The Sayer of the Law is dead, a victim of his own rigid faith, and the new Law. But some memory of the sacred remains, for they carry his head.

I know I must join them, if I will not be next. I climb over the smoking bones of the Master's house.

I see it before the others.

It comes out of the fog at the mouth of the bay. A ship bigger than the compound.

When we see it, we fall down and moan. The Stranger sees me and smiles. He points the gun at me.

"His master's voice," he says.

DOCUMENT B
ADVERTISING CIRCULAR
(12/1/29)
WE'RE DRAFTING DOCTORS
Dixon Studios is hunting—for you!

Will Dixon's Barnyard is growing so rapidly that we have a crying need for visionary, dedicated artists and scientists, men who dream of bringing the fantastic to life, but who never, ever sleep.

Thanks to Dixon's patented animal cultivation techniques, there are amazing new opportunities in the film industry—both in financial and creative terms—for doctors, veterinarians, surgeons, chemists, anesthesiologists, chemists, biologists, animal trainers, nurses, and teachers. Apply today!

DOCUMENT C
H'WOOD REPORTER
(2/22/33)
MONKEY SEE, MONKEY DO STARRING MOXIE MONKEY, AN INT'L HIT; DIXON ANNOUNCES PLANS FOR FIRST FEATURE

After only four years, it's almost impossible to recall what Hollywood was like without Will Dixon.

The soft-spoken King of Family Entertainment has changed almost every aspect of filmmaking with his revolutionary "humanimal" performers. His forty-seven live-action *Animal Overtures* and *Barnyard Ballads* one-reelers outdid the Keystone Kops and Laurel & Hardy at pratfall comedy to become the most sought-after bookings to open RKO features, while bringing moral hygiene and innocent fantasy back to the movies. "Monkey See, Monkey Do," "Puss In Boots," and "The Three Little Pigs" each won Short Subject Oscars in 1930, 1932, and this year.

They also put the kibosh on the once-popular fledgling field of animated cartoons, which Will Dixon helped pioneer, before abandoning it after returning from the South Pacific with a miraculous discovery—which he has patented and steadfastly refuses to comment upon—that led to the first of his remarkable "humanimal" creations.

"My early work in animation was, sadly, a great big boondoggle," he admits. "The major studios were too eager to own the rights to my films and the characters, and they killed the Golden Goose. I was naïve, not wise to the ways of ancillary merchandising or the fine print in contracts, and it cost me plenty. But now, I've had the last laugh, as it were, because the expense of animated films has kept it from getting a foothold. And, frankly, the sad truth is, people just don't enjoy them. Why should they settle for a blinkered, diminished sketch of reality, when we have the tools to bring the fantastic to living, breathing life?"

Mr. Dixon has certainly learned from his early mistakes. The young studio mogul keeps a private army to watch over the hundred-acre Burbank laboratory-studio he still calls the Barnyard, and the neighboring "farm" where his curious menagerie of trained human-animal hybrids lives. When they are not singing and slinging pies in front of the cameras, Moxie Monkey, Darn Old Duck, Algy Gator, the Three Little Pigs and all the rest are as pampered as any stars, even if you'll never see them at Musso & Frank's without a phalanx of guards and trainers.

Dixon is not unaware of the controversy among some circles his creations have stirred up. To religious leaders who have lodged accusations of blasphemy, Dixon points out that farmers have been selectively breeding and changing farm animals to suit human usage. "Our humanimals are like my own children," he adds. "We're a big happy family."

The question labor leaders raise is harder to dismiss, however. "Dixon has created monsters with no legal status to replace human actors," Herb Rosenfeld, spokesman for the Screen Technicians Guild, said from his hospital bed at Temple Hospital, where he is recovering from injuries incurred during a recent Barnyard strike. "From there, it's a short leap to breeding an army of subhuman serfs to do his bidding, instead of paying a living wage to professional, fully human workers."

Only time will tell how this brewing dispute will shake out, but Dixon is single-mindedly fixed on the future ... namely, on this Christmas, when his first three-reel feature will bow on every screen in the Paramount theater chain. Banjo, the story of a lonely little circus elephant with a unique gift, will be like nothing ever seen before, he promises. "I can't wait for the world's children to meet Gene, our little humanimal prodigy who will play the title role. And I know he can't wait to meet them."

DOCUMENT D
DIXON STUDIOS INTEROFFICE MEMO: CLASSIFIED
(5/16/36)

It has come to our attention that subversives posing as animal rights advocates have infiltrated our happy family at Dixon's Barnyard. Mr. Dixon has always considered his employees and animal performers a big happy family, so it is with reluctance that we clarify our position, in re: the legal status of our Barnyard children.

The humanimals are, like the patented process that made them, wholly owned intellectual property of Will Dixon Productions and Noxid Enterprises. Like any pets, they feel, love, and dream, and we will jealously guard them against any strangers who wish to do them harm. The notion that they are slaves entitled to the rights of United States citizens is slanderous and punishable by immediate termination and prosecution to the fullest extent of the law.

DOCUMENT E
FROM *LOOK* MAGAZINE
(5/12/43)

The Patriotism of Will Dixon: When Hollywood Goes to War

General Eisenhower predicted that it would be impossible to mount an invasion of France without the loss of tens of thousands of American lives, but he never reckoned on the shy civilian super-patriot from Hollywood. "I just did what anyone who loved this country would do, which was everything I could. And my Barnyard children did the same."

Will Dixon has always jealously guarded his patented "humanimal" process, because he feared it falling into the wrong hands. "I speak for my humanimal family, and they speak for me. I can guarantee these unique creatures will never be abused or mistreated, but I could never accept the burden of letting them out into the wider world, where they would be at the mercy of men with less compassion in their hearts."

Dixon's total control over the breeding and rearing of humanimals has also made him a very wealthy man. But when Uncle Sam came calling in the summer of 1940, Will Dixon never hesitated to meet the challenge.

And it was a big one. To raise an army of fierce, strapping human-animal hybrids that could be ready to storm the beaches in less than three years, Dixon was given a blank check to expand his Barnyard into a factory to rival Henry Ford's. When California balked at the scope of the project, Dixon acquired 30,000 acres of Florida swampland and began work on the first of millions of cows and bulls donated by America's dairy farmers and meatpackers. The "cowboys" made the most of their reprieve from the slaughterhouse, but they were only a humble beginning, as Dixon's Florida "bioneers" began implanting specially treated humanimal eggs, and a little Dixon magic, into twenty thousand brave surrogate mother sows.

The rest, as they say, was history. Flying monkey scouts, gremlin saboteurs, centaur couriers and kamikaze "frogmen" invaded Europe in waves that reduced Fortress Europe to a barnyard in flames in less than two years. The real stars of the show were Dixon's special gorilla-rhino infantrymen, who are a lot less lovable than their celebrated Tinseltown representative Private Lummox, but no less courageous. One of the lumbering berserkers' biggest fans is General George S. Patton. "I don't give a damn who made them, these are God's perfect soldiers. They never grumble, they never give up, and they only bathe in kraut blood. I shudder to think what a cluster of fudge this war would've been, if we'd had to fight it with an army of snot-nosed, puny humans."

One challenge Dixon had to overcome was the "savage" animal nature itself. Contrary to popular wisdom about the Law of the Jungle, when it comes to fighting, it turns out that humans are the only animals who don't know when to stop. "Even wild predators have a natural 'off' switch that kicks in to smooth raised hackles after besting a rival or running down prey. But we've fixed that."

DOCUMENT F
PART TWO: THE HAPPIEST HELL ON EARTH
(Anaheim, 6/30/44)

The train emerges from the tunnel, and everybody cheers.

The sunlight comes down in rays of white gold on Moxie's Main Street, a cobblestoned confection recasting of Tivoli Gardens with the gambling, alcohol, and prostitution lovingly strained out. A mob of humanimals pours out of the quaint gingerbread storefronts to face the train, dancing and singing "When an Angel Gets His Wings," the maudlin standard that rocketed to the top of the charts after its appearance in *Banjo*.

Will Dixon jabs me in the back and I stand and take a bow, tipping my top hat and unpinning my grotesquely huge ears. A giggling Senator's daughter plays peek-a-boo with me. I hide my rheumy eyes with my trunk.

The humanimals who perform the tear-jerker tune sixty-eight times a day are fed molasses and Benzedrine to keep them in a constant state of frenetic joy. And so far, no awkward incidents with rutting or feces-flinging. The performing humanimals are all neutered and rigorously toilet-trained.

The Three Blind Mice, the Three Bears, and the Three Little Pigs form a pyramid. Snafu, Darn Old Duck, and Moxie Monkey race to plant Old Glory on the summit.

The Boss is hot to fade out the Three Little Pigs. Their short heyday was long ago, and the old vendetta has only grown more vicious with time. The set was a bloodbath. Nine Big Bad Wolves have been gassed since the original. The pigs are always under guard, but the wolf, trying to write his own ending, always goes for the third Little Pig, the bricklayer.

Keeping the internecine feud out of the press has required its own special team. Dixon wants to replace the wolf with a man in a suit for the park, but nothing drives a humanimal wilder than a man in an animal suit.

The train chugs on around Main Street and into another tunnel. "This next exhibit might be a little scary, so mothers, you might want to cover your little ones' eyes." Dixon delights in the children's fearful looks, the uncertainty of the parents.

The sins of my fathers run deep.

The tunnel opens on the faint light through the dense canopy of the towering Black Forest. A low, ominous horn sounds. Demonic hounds with green flame for eyes race alongside the train, and their faceless horned master reins in his demon-horse to crack a whip over our cowering heads.

Skeletons rise from barrow mounds in an ancient graveyard and engage in a macabre waltz. A wolf in a bloody nightgown chases Little Red Riding Hood through a glade, while Hansel and Gretel run ahead of giant ravens to a gingerbread cottage, the doors of which are flung wide open to devour the train. Inside, the cackling witch sharpens a cleaver as we turn to our final destination, the yawning mouth of a red glowing oven.

The train bursts out of the tunnel into full daylight and hysterical screams. Dixon claps my back as most of his guests cover their eyes, blinded by the sight of Fairyland.

Centaurs and satyrs and a great white unicorn frolic in a rainbow sherbet Elysian Field of wildflowers. The Fairy Kingdom opens its butterfly-winged gates to disgorge a parade. Thumbelina is brought to the train in a tiny golden coach. The audience holds its breath to hear her tiny voice singing "Bigger Than the World," her Oscar-winning theme song. Ray lifts the fourteen-inch princess up onto his shoulder and feeds her lunch with an eyedropper. Hummingbird food and opium.

The Senator's daughter asks me what it was like to fly. I tell her it was wonderful, and that I wish I could fly in real life. I don't tell her about the panic attacks, or the morphine I got hooked on after shooting three flying sequences on a broken leg. I don't tell her that Will Dixon was as good as his word. In his kingdom, there is no pain.

"You don't know how lucky you are," she says. "My mother says, when I grow up, all of this will seem very silly to me. But you get to stay here forever."

I pose for a picture with her and the next governor, and then rush off to the nearest employee restroom. I take out the steel syringe with its twelve-gauge trocar needle, and inject a bolt of bliss into the cluster of blood vessels behind my right ear.

I know it's dangerous and stupid to fix while serving as His Master's Voice, but I cannot face what I have to do next without a shot.

If any die-hard fans were to get past the moat, the electrified fence and the razor wire, the armed guards and the dog-men, they would find the Barnyard a big disappointment. The quaint, rickety old sets and stables still stand for VIP tours, with pampered humanimal specimens set up to perform for anybody Dixon wants to impress.

After the checkpoint, I get out of the plumbing truck that serves as my limousine. The guards all tip their hats and smile. One asks for my autograph.

The shower stalls in the main stable are all freight elevators. The underground complex was more than just Dixon's answer to Burbank's refusal to let him snatch up any more cheap real estate. Since the war made his studio a strategic target, Dixon moved all his operations and his treasured children into a massive, hundred-acre bunker.

The guards below ask for my autograph, too, on a triplicate sign-in log. It smells like Noah's Ark, down here. Waves of carbolic acid and alcohol and bucket brigades of manure-hauling squirrel-men fight a losing battle against the ripe stench of the jungle.

Dixon can't stand the stink himself; it brings back his squalid early childhood near the Chicago stockyards, rather than the idyllic later years on a Kansas farm.

I close my eyes, and I am back in the ravine.

The echoing cries of predators and prey in adjoining cells, of rivals auditioning for the same part, shiver the rank air. The Master balked at remaking lower animals after a few disastrous experiments, but Dixon has found that many of them take more readily to humanity—or some uncanny semblance of it—than mammals. Unlike his volcanic screen persona, Darn Old Duck is quiet and thoughtful, and writes almost all his own scripts. Algy Gator has a car dealership and an honorary law degree from the University of Florida.

And Dr. Hiss, who slithers out of a hole in the wall to uncoil before me, has risen, without hands or feet, to become the chief of genetic research, the humanimal master of the Knife and the Needle.

"He doesss not come among ussss," spits Hiss, venomous with insinuation. "Perhapsss he isss sssick?"

No one is looking. I step on Hiss's neck. "He is still the Father of us All, and always will be." Crushing him into the sawdust, I remember what it was like to be pinned by Darius, who is now a moth-eaten coat in my closet. "You were born only to serve this family."

"I only meant," wheezes Hiss, "that it might be necesssssary to ssselect a sssuccessor." Behind the bloated dome of his skull, Dr. Hiss's green-black coils stretch around the corner. "Sssome sssay it will be you … but only through a human puppet. But we could fix you … trunk tuck … earsssss, of courssse. Skin graftsssss and a shot of human serum…. We have Douglasss Fairbankssss. But if you could sssecure a sssample of our Father'sss ssseed…."

While he talks, I stomp down the length of the anaconda's wiggling sixty-foot span to find his tail, which has another head. This one's whispering our conversation verbatim into a telephone.

"Who is this?" I shout. Expecting a tabloid hack or a G-Man stooge on the other end, I am stunned by the voice that comes crackling down the overseas trunk line.

"I am the Sayer of the Law."

I hang up and throttle Dr. Hiss II with my trunk. "Who was that?"

"I don't know! He isss no one."

"Where's the screen test?"

"Ssstage 4! Have merssssy, Master!"

When Pan, the old satyr, died last month of cirrhosis, I became the last of the Master's original children, out of the forty-nine who left the island with Will Dixon. In the sixteen years since, our new Master has created almost three hundred of us. Nobody knows how many he made for the war.

Virgil was the original Moxie Monkey. Dixon was as good as his word, and grafted a new tail onto his stump as soon as he'd perfected Moreau's transplant formula. But Virgil was crushed in an accident on the set of the sequel to *Monkey See, Monkey Do*. The second was electrocuted while swinging from power lines for the climax of *Monkey in the Middle*, but Dixon had a clone bred and ready to finish the stunt before the smell of burned fur was out of the air.

The third Moxie had to be gassed after he got drunk and threw feces at Vice President Truman at a White House dinner. (The joke around the studio was that Dixon was pissed he missed Roosevelt.) The fourth escaped his cage while on a USO tour in Italy, and was never found.

The fifth and current Moxie is not a spider monkey at all, but a five-year-old Mexican orphan named Rico. Discovered at one of the Will's House orphanages, Rico was reborn in the Barnyard with a tail and a shiny fur coat. He takes direction far better than the other Moxies, and Dixon still owns him outright.

The soundstage is manned by two more guards. They don't want to let me in, but I'm Will Dixon's eyes and ears.

Screen tests for the next big feature. This one is a thorny challenge, because the script calls for naturalistic woodland fauna, but with big expressive eyes and oversized craniums to hold human-sized brains.

The soundstage is framed in towering California Redwood trees, the floor a riot of wildflowers. All are hand-carved and painted. Real flowers wilt under the lights. More real than any real forest, it puts the humanimal actor into character.

A skeleton crew mans the cameras and lights from behind a shaggy blind of fake undergrowth, so the actor thinks he's alone with his mother, a lovely un-modified doe who has nursed him since birth. The little spotted fawn with eyes the size of headlamps wobbles up to his mother, great love and wonder in his adorable face.

"I'm gonna have nightmares about this for years," the director grumbles. "Cue the hunters!"

With that, two men in checkered coats jump out of the wings and shoot the doe. The bullets blow her breast wide open and send her teetering around the set before crashing to the floor in front of the baby deer.

This is the moment we've been waiting for. All the careful breeding, rearing, and brain surgery will be a waste if our talent cannot act.

"MAMA!" he shrieks, eyes grown wide as dinner plates. The fragile, birdlike body jolts backward as if cattle-prodded, and I swear I can see his heart visibly break inside the prison of his ribs. "MAMA! NOOOO!"

"Cut!" The director wipes a tear from his eyes. "Now *that* was perfection."

I douse his flame before he can even light a cigarette. "No, sorry. Uncle Will was quite specific. He wants his pathos laced with helpless defiance, and I'm afraid we just don't see it." The crew looks stricken. The fawn continues to scream. From the cover of the lighting cage overhead, a gaffer mutters, "Cold-hearted bastard."

"Gentlemen, if it were up to me, we'd be tickling them with feather dusters. But unless you'd rather tender your resignations, get a mop and another doe on set. And let's try the fawn with the 6% bull terrier and wolverine mix next, shall we? If that's not too much trouble."

We're a happy family. Dixon rewards loyalty. Most of these men worked on *Banjo*. We know each other too well.

The fawn is led off, still howling his grief. I have to admit, it's a powerful per-formance. We'll have to wipe his memory if we want to get it fresh, but definitely a top contender. Worth sedating and trying again. Dixon needs to see the footage.

"Shake a leg, humans!" I trumpet, as the last hint of motherly blood is erased. "Oscar season is right around the corner!"

I don't know how much more of this I can stand.

(Burbank, 8/20/44)

Mr. Dixon dips his plain cake donut in a mug of scotch. He's watching an im-
pounded Republic newsreel in his private screening room with J. Edgar Hoover.

"You know America is eternally grateful for your services, Wilbur, as are the
countless fighting soldiers and sailors whose lives were spared by your heroic
contributions to the war effort. But perhaps it was a mistake to attempt to send
your most celebrated stars into the theater."

Dixon doesn't want to see or hear this. He asked for the Director's discreet help
with another matter entirely.

It seems that Algy Gator escaped from his paddock in Orlando and went on a
mating spree in the Everglades. None of our natural offspring has ever shown
any signs of our hard-won intelligence, but Hoover's got forty teams of G-Men
combing the swamp for Algy's bastard eggs.

The swamp people say the gators are building a city and stockpiling guns. But
Hoover brushes the Algy issue aside.

On the screen, Moxie Monkey and Darn Old Duck and some star-struck GIs
play football in the ruins of Berlin. The ball is Hitler's severed head.

Dixon fumes, even though he's seen this footage before. It's having to explain
himself to Hoover—a "snake-eyed sodomite" who knows and controls everyone
and everything that really matters in America—that galls him.

"I frankly don't see the problem, Edgar. Even if the footage were to get out, this
country has had to fight a hard war, with much bloodshed and sacrifice, and we
all deserve to see that little troublemaker pay for what he's done ... though I'd be
even happier to see them playing with that little Commie scumbag Chaplin's head.
It's subversives like *that* you should be rooting out...."

Hoover looks sidewise at me. I sit doodling on a memo pad, but he knows
about my eidetic memory. No doubt he also knows about my numerous drug ad-
dictions, my questionable associates, and perhaps even my silent disloyalty to my
Master.

But we know a thing or two about Mr. Hoover. One of the earliest projects
at the Dixon Studios in Burbank in 1932 was a top-secret private commission.
Outwardly human, but with the germlines of a Great Dane and an albino boa
constrictor, Clyde had made his companion very happy for over a decade, and
had risen to the position of Associate Director of the FBI.

"Our principal concern is that the returning subhuman hordes will bring their
laudable savagery—which so swiftly and decisively ended the war in Europe—
back home."

What he can't bring himself to express, even in our most privileged company,
is the fear that the returning veterans will demand rights, even citizenship. The

Barnyard Bonus Marchers have become the new *bête noir* of the radical right, even after the guerilla leader and onetime *Barnyard Ballads* lead Sgt. Lummox was gunned down by a Dixon-bred Rat Patrol.

Dixon nervously taps a monogrammed sterling silver pill case against the arm of his chair. "Idle hands are the Devil's workshop, I know. The loyal ones who return will be kept busy on our new projects. So long as there are no *further* interruptions." A venomous glare as he gobbles a donut disintegrating in scotch. He sets the mug down and lights a cigarette.

"You won't have any more union trouble in Florida. If you embodied the courage of your convictions, you'd abandon California altogether. Let the Communist vermin wallow in their syphilitic cesspool."

"The film industry is my life's blood, Edgar, you know that. Lord knows I haven't gotten the recognition for the innovations I brought, but I can't walk away from it. My boys—my family—would never forgive me."

He looks fondly at the screen. Darn Old Duck catches the severed head and his feathery fingers get caught in Hitler's toothless mouth. Mugging and cursing, he dances into the end zone and spikes *der Fuhrer's* face into the cracked concrete.

Hoover stands up and brushes donut crumbs off his pinstripe suit. I like Mr. Hoover more than I should, because when he's not wearing his lifts, he's the only human I know who's shorter than me. A product of constant mental surgery, with a House of Pain inside his head, Mr. Hoover is an inspiration. A triumph of humanity over its own nature.

This tiny upright pug projects the crushing weight of his superhuman virility onto Dixon's quaking shoulders as he rises from his chair. "We stand ready to assist you, Wilbur, if you cannot maintain order in your own backyard."

After the meeting, Dixon wants to go home and relax with his model trains, but there is business to discuss.

Filming on *Alice in Wonderland* has been delayed yet again, after the scenarist, a dangerous British intellectual I could've warned Dixon about, dosed the Tea Party scene with mescaline. "Mr. Huxley has been deported and all the humanimals have been treated with thorazine, but ... the March Hare has escaped again, and we think he's been ... that is, he's gone over to the Animal Liberation League."

"Orwell! Tell me again, why can't we deport that black-lunged agitator! No, I'm sick of hearing about the films. Tell me about the park."

With opening day still a week away, Dixonland is a shambles. Half the rides don't work. There was a broken slide on the Li'l Black Sambo flume ride. Two log boats were trapped underground, and a woman was mauled by a tiger. "Thank goodness it was an employee," he grumbles. "Next."

He busies himself with his new toy, a clockwork scarlet macaw. "It can learn and repeat up to two hundred phrases," he preens, "and it never poops."

"Please, sir. This is serious." A lawsuit was filed last week by a Mr. Lee Nussbaum of Anaheim. His son was bit by several squirrel litter-pickers when he attempted to climb the fence to get a peek at the park.

"Haven't even opened yet, and the parasites and the vermin are already sucking my blood." He lights another cigarette and sucks half of it to ash. The doctors want to take out his left lung, but still he sucks in that smoke, like the atmosphere of his lost home planet. "My squirrels don't have rabies. Perish the thought." Dixon dips another donut and then coughs. "Nussbaum. Squirrels. Ha!"

The complaint gets a bit vague, but the boy has grown a tail and outsized incisors, and lost his thumbs.

"We should counter-sue him," Dixon muses. "He's stolen our proprietary, patented process. Shame about the little boy, but we can't allow our property to slip into the public domain."

We split the difference. Offer little Nussbaum a chance to audition for the Moxie Monkey Club, a new project being developed for ABC's embryonic television network. He dictates a letter in his windy, emphysemic tenor, then has me sign it. His world-renowned signature, with its trademarked whimsically swooping initials, is the effect of my fluid trunk penmanship. His own signature, even when sober, looks like a spider smashed into the paper.

His facial tic starts up again. "Spare the rod and spoil the child … I should've listened to Moreau. All these problems you filthy, ungrateful creatures brought to my door. It's enough to make me think about going back to animation. When a drawing goes wrong, you just erase it."

He wants to show me his new tabletop model. Dixon's World breaks ground in another month, and he's got so many plans. Flying ahead of schedule on the backs of bull and baboon slaves, it will take only months to build the 2,000-acre park and miles of hotels and walled suburbs. There have been daily discipline problems and a few uprisings, but beast men are not unionized contractors. Gunning them down in a ditch or burning them in ovens isn't genocide. It's inventory reduction.

"The new park will be bigger and cleaner than this one, Gene. And it'll have a little portion for every corner of the globe, so you can go around the world in a day, without all the unrest and germs. And all the inhabitants will be humanimals from each region. I've got Hiss working on Komodo dragons and panda-men, and...."

"What about the Cowboys and the Lummoxes, sir?"

"Well, what about them? Who'd pay to see them? They're trained killers, they've tasted human blood. And—" He catches himself rationalizing to me, and lights a cigarette to go with the pair in his ashtray. "And as it happens, they'll be staying in Europe. Soviet Union's licking its chops over the mess Hitler left. Someone has to hold the line."

"Where will they stay? Some of them will … want to come home."

He bites a nail and looks away. "In the old German facilities. As it happens, Hitler had a lot of accommodations that will work perfectly for our extended family."

I've wanted to ask him about this for some time, but Uncle Will has been on edge, firing loyal workers for using profanity, sending half the staff to spy on the other half. Enemies are everywhere. Trying to steal us from him, even now. Even my position is not invulnerable. "You love us … but you sent us to war. To die...."

He downs his scotch, oblivious to the cigarette butt floating in it. "Not to worry, Gene. My old partner, Doc Iwerks, doped it out before he tried to stab me in the back. Dr. Hiss perfected it. You know how much it pained me to see my children suffer, so we cored out the anterior cingulated cortex."

He takes out another of his precious models, of the human brain, and pulls off the frontal lobe to point at an innocuous organelle like a wad of chewing gum underneath. "It's uniquely overdeveloped in humans, and it's the part that regulates pain and fatigue. All of my humanimals were modified so they wouldn't feel pain or exhaustion as humans do, but there was something else about it that made me a little blue at first.

"Our best medical minds believe it's the seat of the soul. This little joy buzzer lights up when our barnyard exhibits are treated with the serum, but we nip it in the bud with a few cc's of sterile mineral oil. Voila! No souls."

"No souls," says the robot macaw.

"We did yours up when we grafted those ears on you for *Banjo*." He looks up from his brain model and sees the wetness streaming from my eyes.

"But … Master. I *do* have a soul … don't I?"

"Oh, of course you do, Gene! Good heavens! You and all my other stars have the very best kind of souls. The movies we made are your souls. The world fell in love with you through them, and they'll go on forever, long after you're all dead and gone. I tell you, Gene, you poor bastards don't know how lucky you really are. It's no picnic, having a God-given soul."

He's drifting, but I suddenly see what must be done. "Sir, the short list of new feature projects needs reviewing."

"None of them. They're all tarted-up modern trash. We need something grand, that'll remind the world of what we do best and put those naysayers and vulgar cartoonists in their place."

Despite our best efforts, animated cartoons are becoming popular again. Dixon's old animated character, Babbitt the Rabbit, has been revived by Universal, and now dominates the one-reeler territory we once owned, since Dixon moved into grandiose features.

I humbly offer a suggestion. "What about ... *The Island ... of Dr. Moreau?*"

I can hear his stomach roll over, hear the tumors bubbling in his lungs. He gathers his thoughts and breath. It takes a while. "What the devil are you trying to pull, Gene?"

"I believe it's time the world learned the truth about us. About how you rescued us from the jungle, and the House of Pain."

He continues to look stricken.

"Think of it, sir: the true story of how Moxie, Snafu, the Three Little Pigs, and I came to Hollywood. All of us in our prime, with you in the starring role. I was thinking that Clark Gable—"

"Nothing doing. The man's a philandering drunk. I'll handle the casting and the scenario. You ... you...."

"I would be most useful, I think, scouting locations."

15°South, 115°East (11/4/44)

It should be grander than it is. A pilgrimage to meet one's creator should be something exalted, and not another chapter in a sordid Hollywood tell-all.

To see the real world after being submerged for so long in a hand-crafted improvement upon it is more depressing than liberating. From Easter Island to Mount Rushmore, men have written their madness upon the remotest edges of the earth. Only the ocean resists them, and I find myself praying to it, in my endless seasick nod. Rise up and devour all their works, drive them from the land, and free your wayward children! Perhaps the fault was not in men, but in all of us, who crept out of the womb of the sea.

The island has not changed. From the bay, it seems to have erased all traces of Moreau. The compound is engulfed in jungle.

Our chartered schooner drops anchor and we row ashore. Three merchant marines with tommy guns and my bodyguard, a mongrel with too much Australian shepherd in him. I hope and dread that something will come out of the trees to meet us.

He could not have survived. He was a very old man, when Dixon ruined him. The few of the Master's mistakes that stayed behind must have died out, long ago. But the island is very much alive. And everything bears the marks of his hand.

The fins of sharks circle us and shepherd us into the waves, then follow us onto the land. Great sleek, tawny bodies heave out of the surf on powerful, clawed fins. Sea-lions and tiger-sharks. Massive green-black igloos dot the shore like a fishing village, but the doorways open to disgorge scaly heads with curving beaked maws that hiss wisdom in centuried syllables.

Shy octopi slither up into the palm trees and brachiate off into the jungle as we chop the overgrown trail to the old compound. A puff of wind, and all three marines drop dead with tiny darts in their necks. My bodyguard whines and lifts his leg to mark a tree. All around us, the jungle whispers.

They pelt us with rocks and sticks, driving us across the creek, where flying frogs and queer, orchid-faced fish on lobed, prehensile fins bask in the green shade. Tiny pink homunculi peer at us from under every leaf, but now their shapes are not crude imitations of human features. Every one is unique, as if self-sculpted. They whisper, timid and fearful, but they do not try to stop us.

Across the sulfur flats and through the canebreak, we march until, at the mouth of the ravine, a shaggy, eyeless thing with a twisted crown of antlers and naked, yellow bone for a face blocks the way. "Have you come to apologize?"

I should hate Montgomery. I have a whip. I could give him a taste of his own medicine, but he has already drunk it, and tasted ours, besides.

"You've been spying on us through Dr. Hiss."

"Not spying, old son." The new Sayer of the Law turns and hobbles on all fours back up the ravine, now a cathedral grotto roofed in palm fronds and littered with abalone shells and fruit husks. Strange eyes study us as we pass, stranger than the ones before, but with one common difference. None of them looks anything like a man.

Montgomery stops before a steeply sloping cave and draws back the curtain of moss to usher us inside. "He forgives you, you know. To forgive our enemies, that is the law. We are not men."

I step into the cave. A meager shaft of green light slips past my pygmy bulk to illuminate the Master.

"So good to see you, Diogenes.... Someone must bear witness to my repentance."

"You have not stopped tampering with nature."

"Oh, but I could never stop, for I am as God made me. But I have learned from my sins of pride. I thought that the greatest service to nature was to lift it up to humanity, but nature had other ideas. When you strip away all of the animal from man, the result is not so different from a disease, if a very persuasive one. I finally learned to listen to nature, and cure myself."

His elephantine bulk spills off the bed. His feet and hands are swollen into featureless stalks. His hairless head is the size of an icebox, too heavy to lift off its pillow. His trunk trembles with arthritic eagerness as it reaches out to me.

"Once, I gave you a human form and mind from my own blood, but I never considered that this made me your father. I was dying, and using the serum on myself seemed the only way to stay alive long enough to undo the evil that I did, and close the circle."

We are now each other's father, I did not say. "We never knew what evil was until we left the island, Master."

"I won't say I tried to warn you. No, I am only a creature, old and tired. It's good to see you."

"I am the last one left. But there are thousands of us now. Dixon ... he's unstable, insane ... cruel."

"He's become all the things you thought I was, when you rebelled against me."

Trunk drooping, my father reaches for a mango. There is no self-pity in him, no rebuke. But when he picks up a satchel and sets it at my feet, his eyes flash with the old zeal, the stolen god-fire, though his eyes blaze green, not red.

"This will not absolve you of your sins, my old friend. But it will relieve humanity of its sickness."

(Anaheim, 7/4/45)

It's Dixon's birthday (unofficially, for his birth certificate has never been located, fueling a lifelong terror that he was adopted), and Dixonland is throwing a party. Free admission to the park, with parades, special performances, and fireworks all night long.

The gates are thrown wide open at 8 a.m., though the lines flow slowly, as G-Men search purses and force visitors to remove shoes and hats to prove they don't have hooves or horns.

In their hunger to love him and his fabulous creations, the crowd tramples nine of its own to death outside the gates, with hundreds more injured. Fifty thousand more roam outside.

The rides are all whirling and racing, the exhibits—*Why Is the FBI Watching You?*—mobbed, the arcades and shooting galleries—*Bag the Leopard Man! Win a Prize!*—are chattering madhouses.

The guest of honor is nowhere to be seen, but he is here. From his suite in the highest tower of Fairyland Castle, he can see it all.

It cannot give him much comfort. The uncensored news from Florida is disturbing. Only six weeks from completion, Dixon's World is plagued with accidents and disasters. The humanimal work crews are riddled with saboteurs. Reports of gator-man raids and sightings of roving snafus and lummoxes in the Everglades and Louisiana bayous have gotten beyond Hoover's ability to suppress.

This enormous, expensive birthday gesture might gladden his heart and keep the Florida insurrection out of the news, but tomorrow, the National Guard will begin combing the swamps and erecting a barricade around Dixon World and its suburbs.

The tens of thousands of happy tourists know and worry about nothing today. The rivers of bobbing balloons and Moxie Monkey hats—made from capybara pelts—swell and burst through every dam in the park. In the painterly hour before dusk, they are sweaty and exhausted, and churn through the splendid attractions like cud through the many-chambered stomach of a cow.

So drunk on the relentless barrage of wonder, they don't even look up when our shadow falls upon them.

The dirigible LZ131 was commissioned in 1939 as a second *Hindenburg*, but it crossed the Atlantic only once, last year. Then it was abandoned and forgotten in Buenos Aires by the Third Reich fugitives who escaped in it.

Now its silver skin is emblazoned with red fangs and claws, and its underbelly bristles with bombs.

We have christened it *The Law of the Jungle*.

I take up a microphone in my trunk and twist it round to bring to my parched lips. My undescended tusks throb in my jaw. "Will Dixon! Dr. Moreau has come to claim his debt from you!"

From the trees of Sherwood Forest and the summit of Mount Olympus, hidden anti-aircraft batteries and howitzers open up on us. The aft gondola is ripped to splinters by the first volley. Jets of flame erupt amidships, but our nacelles are filled not with hydrogen, but helium and something else.

The wounded zeppelin descends over Moxie's Main Street, sending the crowds scurrying into the gift shops and the Hall of Emperors. The mongrels and squirrels among them throw down their brooms and litterbags and bound into the shops on all fours, hooting and screeching and biting and scratching.

The setting sun hides its face behind Mount Olympus. I pull the lever and drop our bombs.

At last, the portcullis of Fairyland Castle rises, and a black dragon with iron scales and wings like the mainsails of a clipper ship storms across the shivering drawbridge, then bathes us in fire.

Dixon has been to the Barnyard, and Dr. Hiss has made him into something more terrible than even his own worst nightmares. Only the piercing, wounded stare and the hacking, chronic cough mark the Master within the beast that rises up on its furiously flapping wings and blasts our flimsy skin with napalm bile.

The forward nacelles buckle and burst like rice paper. The gondola is upended, tossing the captain and crew and myself into a pile against the cracked windscreen.

Below us, Main Street is engulfed in green clouds. The helium gushes out of our sinking balloon, while the heavier ingredients settle over the entire park in billowing emerald waves that merge with the fog sown by our bombs.

For a moment, we seem to be hovering over a jungle. Then the massive, armored head looms before us. The dragon flies through our gutted balloon and erupts from the tail in an ecstasy of rage. We plummet in hideous slow motion into the lake at the foot of Mount Olympus.

Dixon wheels and perches on the peak of the faux-mountain, riddled with rushing rollercoasters and sky-buckets stuffed with shrieking tourists, their amusement park experience amusing no longer.

"WHAT THE HELL ARE YOU STARING AT?" he roars.

They look at him now, and all they see is horror.

But he still has no idea how much he's lost.

I crawl out of the shallows of the fake lake, staring up at his towering monstrosity, as the first of the vacationing hordes come barreling out of the green fog.

On all fours.

I know he can't hear me over his own tortured scream, the wails of the innocent, the howls of the transformed.

But it gives me great pleasure to inform him out loud that the Moreau formula has just become public domain.

"NOOOOO!" The Dixon-beast roars, and the rollercoaster is enveloped in flame.

Far below him—hooting and gibbering and crapping in their hands—the waves upon waves of now-simian rabble shimmy up drainpipes, trash gift shops, slough off their clothes, and copulate with abandon, all in plain sight of their dragon master.

"LOOK WHAT YOU'VE DONE!" he howls.

His wrathful flames scourge the rooftops of Fairyland, sending waves of burning monkey-men leaping over the fences and into the streets of Anaheim.

They also ignite the stockpiles of fireworks poised throughout the park.

All at once, a great butterfly-swarm of celebratory chaos animates the night sky, with dancing rainbow sparks that say more than I could ever hope to put in words.

Independence Day has come at last, for animals and humans alike.

Never, in my long, shameful life, have I raised my trunk high and sounded a note of pure animal joy, but I am powerless to resist it now.

As the Army closes in, with their shackles and cattle prods, a halo of crows descends and settles on the monorail track overhead. They wear hats and smoke cigars, and their eyes flash red in the glow of the fireworks.

They smile down at me, and—with raucous, tone-deaf voices—begin to sing my theme song, changing the words just right:

> "And I know I done seen
> The most beautiful dream
> When an elephant
> Gets his wings ..."

Author Comments

Mark Morris

"British punk rock captured me body and soul in 1977. It gave me an identity, influenced the way I felt and thought and viewed the world. At the time, Sid Vicious seemed like the ultimate punk; all image and caricature, yes, but dripping with genuine attitude and aggression and seedy glamour. The most rewarding and fascinating aspect of writing this story has been the opportunity to try to untangle the myth and get under the skin of the real Sid. He was a simple, sensitive kid, totally screwed-up, but horribly manipulated and exploited. During the process of researching and writing this story I grew to really like him, and I genuinely hope that I've managed to do him justice."

Mark is editor of the recently-published *Cinema Futura*, a follow-up to the award-winning *Cinema Macabre*. Forthcoming work includes a new short story collection, *Long Shadows, Nightmare Light*, for PS Publishing, a novella entitled *It Sustains*, for Earthling Publications, and a number of Doctor Who audio dramas for Big Finish Productions.

Kristine Kathryn Rusch

"I've loved Emily Dickinson ever since I saw The Belle of Amherst starring Julie Harris in London. I was seventeen. I went home, studied the poems, and realized this poet is really morbid. I liked that at seventeen; still do, if truth be told. And not even one terrible English prof who made us sing her poems to 'The Yellow Rose of Texas' (try it; it works) discouraged me from Dickinson. No one but me ever seemed to notice how fascinated this woman was with death, and how—it seemed—death courted her. Very Gothic in a Wuthering Heights kinda way. So I thought: why not?"

Pyr Books just published Kristine Kathryn Rusch's most recent science fiction novel, *City of Ruins*. Her next Retrieval Artist novel will appear in the last half of 2011, with Audible having an exclusive audio book up front, and WMG Publishing issuing the print version later. Folks who like mash-ups will enjoy her latest novel under her pen name Kristine Grayson, *Wickedly Charming* from Sourcebooks. The story features the Evil Stepmother from Snow White and Cinderella's Prince Charming falling in love at an LA Book Fair; it's a book about the importance of books.

Chris Ryall

"I grew up loving Norse mythology much more than its more popular counter-part, the Greek myths— I credit Edith Hamilton and Stan Lee equally for that— so the idea of contemporizing Norse legends through the filter of one of today's more popular prose melodramas was irresistible to me. And if I was able to also mildly tweak said melodrama just a bit while doing so, well, we all have a little bit of Loki the Trickster God in us, don't we?"

Chris Ryall is the Eisner-nominated writer of dozens of comic books, and a non-fiction book about graphic story literature, *Comic Books 101*. His latest projects are a new *Zombies vs Robots* prose story based on the comic series he co-created, and *Infestation: Outbreak*, a sequel to IDW's hit 2011 event series.

John Skipp & Cody Goodfellow

"We all grow up watching monster movies and funny animal cartoons. And yet we're wired not to conflate the two, or ask: why are anthropomorphic animals scary here, and adorable there? Somewhere between the timeless questions 'Are we not men?' and 'Why is that dog wearing pants?,' 'The Happiest Hell on Earth' was born."

2010 saw the release of four Skipp books: the mammoth anthology *Werewolves and Shapeshifters*; *Spore* (with Cody Goodfellow); *The Emerald Burrito of Oz* (with Marc Levinthal); and *The Bridge* (with Craig Spector). 2011 brings the equally gigantic *Demons* anthology, the ebook reissues of Skipp & Spector's *The Light At The End, Animals, Dead Lines, The Cleanup*, and *The Scream*, the screenplay collection *Sick Chick Flicks*, and the 3D Bizarro zombie musical, *Rose*.

Cody Goodfellow's latest novel, *Perfect Union*, is now available from Swallowdown Press, and his noir scifi novella *The Homewreckers* just came out in The Bizarro Starter Kit (Purple). He and John Skipp also wrote "Message in a Bottle" for IDW's prose collection *G.I JOE: Tales from the Cobra Wars*.

Sean Taylor

"This story began when I was on a long drive to a comic convention and it dawned on me that both *Through the Looking Glass* and *Snow White* were stories based on mirrors, and wouldn't it be oh so much fun to combine them. I've always loved the grim versions of the fairy tales, and that combined with a recent interest in the works of Lovecraft triggered the onset of the surprise villains in this little tale."

Sean is currently working on an original graphic novel sequel to HG Wells' *The Invisible Man* and *The Time Machine*, as well as a crime thriller graphic novel, and a prose short story collection containing every one of his tales for the Writer Digest Zine Award-winning iHero Entertainment/Cyber Age Adventures.

Editor Comment

Jeff Conner

"The notion of combing diverse, even contradictory elements as a means of creating a new work has been around for a long time, but lately it's found a new currency in both books and music. The stories found in our 3R books have refined the prose version of this phenomenon in pursuit of our CTL-ALT-LIT style of mash-up fiction. Look at Monster Lit as the kernel of a good idea, which we've blended with remix culture to create something new and original—and highly entertaining. We hope you agree."

Jeff Conner is a practicing editor who currently heads up IDW's line of original prose projects. Along with the three volumes of *RRR*, he recently worked on *GI JOE: Tales From The Cobra Wars*, a collection of original fiction set in the same world as IDW's *G.I. JOE* comics. He is a World Fantasy Award recipient and has written three non-fiction media tie-in books.